PAMPAS CAT

THE SEQUEL

BY

WILLIAM S. LEET

For Bob
one fine brother

Acknowledgments

Once again, my wife, Mary-Helen, not only found things that needed fixing, but warned me at least once when I was about to get off course. Because of her help, the book is better than it would have been without it, and I herewith thank her for her help as well as for the patience she has for her husband sitting around writing books, often when there are more pressing matters to attend to.

The cover photo is of a painting by Rainbow Touraine.

FOREWORD

If you have not read *Pampas Cat,* I suggest reading it prior to reading this sequel. The story line of this book begins where *Pampas Cat* ended. Thus, readers who have not read *Pampas Cat,* or who do not remember it, will not fully understand the actions, motivations and attitudes of the characters, or even some of the humor in this book. *Pampas Cat* is available for purchase on Amazon, as are my other books. In case these words are not sufficient encouragement to read *Pampas Cat,* the final chapter is included as an Afterword to this book.

It should be obvious that this is a work of fiction. Everything about it is fictional. During my career as a fish biologist, I was involved in the scientific management of fish populations and fish habitat restoration. Professionals around the globe are doing the same, not only for fish and other aquatic life, but for terrestrial wildlife and plant life. I am a strong advocate of protecting the environmental values that have driven the process of evolution toward the broad mix of flora and fauna that presently define the living earth. I find the mythical beliefs that some animal parts have aphrodisiac properties to be repulsive and irresponsible. They *are* myths and they are fueled by the greed of the people who sell the parts for profit.

William Leet

CHAPTER ONE

Although every tiny motion shot daggers of pain through his body, Buford Parker was still struggling to get out of his straitjacket when he was removed from the ambulance at Austin State Hospital.

"Keep still," the huge African American orderly said in a quiet but deep, commanding voice.

"Keep still? You two assholes are hurting me. Lemme outa this god damn thing. You are dealing with Buford Parker, and Buford Parker don't take shit from anybody, heah?"

Austin State Hospital, formerly called the Texas State Lunatic Asylum, was the first such facility to be built west of the Mississippi. It started out in 1861 with twelve patients, and the name was changed in 1925. When Buford arrived the population of psychiatric patients had grown to 250 or so, most, if not all of whom were far more disabled than Parker. After all, Buford was not mentally impaired. Indeed, he was a clever man who had never lived in the main thoroughfare of life but had achieved what he would define as success. He had killed a family of four in Argentina, and had not responded to fatalities caused by his neglect of an apartment complex he owned. He had also poisoned a magnificent Pampas Cat. But he had given hundreds of thousands of dollars to the Texas Longhorns football program, and by being a free-spender was a positive contributor to Austin's economy. In fact he never would have found himself at Austin State if he had not pitched a tantrum when he emerged from his coma (a tantrum, by the

5

way, that even two years later is the subject of much discussion and laughter around the hospital).

The check-in procedure at Austin State involved taking patients through the rec-room. Patients who were not confined to restricted areas spent much of their time in the rec-room, where some sat staring into space, some would antagonize all the others, some would make peculiar noises, many would engage in fictional "projects," and so on. It was a zoo. When Parker was escorted through in his straightjacket the room erupted with cheering, jeering, and more profanity than the profane Mr. Parker had ever heard in a one minute time span.

"I shouldn't be here," he said, trying to act sane. "I am Buford Parker. Did you know that?"

The orderlies did not respond, and Buford's pressure valve exploded in a massive contorted attempt to free himself from the jacket and the orderlies. The pain caused him to scream, which caused a cacophony of noise to erupt in the rec-room – hoots, howls, laughter, and shouting, none of which could be separated by origin, except for one patient repeatedly yelling "fuck you" in his fullest volume. Tears formed in Buford's eyes as he realized his fate. Again he returned to portraying what he believed would appear sane. "Nice bunch of assholes you have here. What did you say your name was? By the way, you have a really good job. What's your name? If we're having a conversation, I should know your name. Yeah, you must love your job, getting to see these assholes every day. *Every day!* You must love it. How do you get a job like this. Think I could get hired on?"

Neither orderly responded, and Buford went limp, necessitating the orderlies to drag him the final few yards to the registration office. Upon entering the office Buford spotted a man sitting at a large dark-stained wooden desk and wearing a Texas Longhorns hat. Hanging on the wall were photographs of Earl Campbell, Vince Young, and Ricky Williams. *Hot damn, now I'm in the right place. Jesus, they don't make it easy to get here, but at least the people who run this place seem to have their priorities in order. They ought to fire these two assholes who brought me in, for Christ's sake. They fucked with Buford Parker.*

One of the orderlies began to say something, and Buford spoke over him. "Hook 'em, baby," he said, extending his index and little fingers. "You're looking at Buford Parker. Whatever the fuck these assholes think they're doing is beyond me, but I'll count on you to straighten it out. Maybe by firing these two nobodies."

Robert "Moon" Muenter was the hospital administrator. "Thanks, Vinnie. Thanks, Doowite," he said. "Have a seat, Mr. Parker."

"Buford Parker. You can call me Buford. Glory be to God, I think the horns are goin' to have a good year. Whadaya think? What's your name, sir?"

"Muenter," said the administrator.

"Well, Muenter, how do you like the Horns? I think they've got a shot at the playoffs. Whadaya think? What's your last name, by the way, Muenter?"

"Muenter."

"Muenter Muenter is your name? Where are you from, the Sudan, or something? Or Samoa? You don't look like it."

Mr. Muenter did not respond to Parker. He merely said to one of the orderlies, "Stick Parker in the tank for a couple days." The tank was what they called the isolation ward.

"Sure, boss," said Doowite, a six-four black man, who had been a tight end at Texas.

"By the way, Muenter. These guys are treating me rough. Especially the nigra. You might want to look into some disciplinary action."

"The African-American man you refer to was all-Big 12 at Texas."

"Doowite Jackson? You're Doowite Jackson? Balls! Sorry to be rude, sir. Maybe I could get your autograph. I've got me a man cave at m' ranch, which you're welcome to visit. Hot damn, I could make your day – or your night, I should say –

7

by slipping you a couple of my magic morsels. Pampas Cat balls. I know you probably don't know what the hell I'm talking about, but you will. I promise you that."

"Take him down to the tank," Muenter said softly.

In a voice barely audible to Parker, Doowite Jackson said, "You behave now, mister, or I'll put my autograph on your face. Around here we don't 'look into disciplinary action,' we just do the discipline. See, we all carry what we call a license to discipline. We don't have no meeting. We don't have no jury trial. We don't have no conference. No mediator. No such shit as that. It's not to say we don't have instruction. We do. It's part of the job training. So the job training is, 'do the discipline as necessary. As necessary. Know what I'm sayin'?"

Buford's heart sank. *These fools don't even know who I am. How in God's name did I ever get into this revolting situation. And that Muenter! What could his hat size be? It must be a ten or so. Oh lordie lordie lordie.*

℘

Three hours after Doowite and Vinnie had left Buford in the tank Muenter's phone rang. "Meunter," he said.

"This is Dr. Tranchini over at Brackenridge. Did your guys get our patient to you all right?"

"Yes, he's here, doctor. Quite a specimen. That's not a medical diagnosis, by the way."

"Is he okay? He just came out of a coma. He's in critical condition. You've got a nurse on duty there 24/7, I know. What about a doctor?"

"Nine to five every weekday. On call on weekends."

"Did they tell you what they thought about Parker?"

"No. They haven't said anything to me."

"They saw him, of course."

"I don't know, doc. It's not SOP if that's what you're asking."

"Would you have your physician give me a call?"

"Sure, doc. What did you say your name is?"

"Tranchini."

Muenter dialed up Doowite Jackson's extension, which was answered with a snappy, "Jackson."

"How's the new guy doing?"

"I dunno. Okay, I guess. The guy sure is pissed off. You'd think he'd never been in a straitjacket before."

"Okay. He's in the tank?"

"Yes, sir."

"Good. Thanks, Doowite."

When Muenter's phone rang two hours later it was Jerome Benson, MD, the staff doctor at Austin State. "Do you have a message for me?" Benson asked.

"No, sir."

"I just talked to Dr. Tranchini over at Brackenridge, and he told me that you were supposed to call me."

"Oh?"

"That's what he said."

"Oh?"

"Did you forget about that?

"It's possible he said something like that. Tranchini, you said?"

"That's right, Moon. Don't give me any shit. Run this place how you want, but when a doctor asks me to call him, pass the message."

"Sorry, doc, it must have slipped through the cracks."

"Bring the new patient up to sick bay."

"He's unruly, doc. We've got him in the tank."

"Muenter, what are you? A retired football coach? Last I heard that's what you were anyway. Or did you get your MD last week?"

"Lighten up. We'll send him up to you."

"God damn it, Muenter, show a little respect to the medical staff. If I ran this place, I'd can your ass."

"I run it, doc, and believe it or not, I could can you. I'll have our boy sent right up."

Muenter rang Doowite and told him to take the patient to sick bay. Two minutes later Muenter's phone rang. It was Doowite. "He's asleep. Should I waken him up?"

"Doowite, wake him up and get him up to Benson."

"I figured you say that, so I already tried to waken him and couldn't."

"Couldn't?

"No, sir. Sound asleep"

"Shit. Get Vinnie and bring him up on a stretcher."

"Ten-four."

"Make haste."

"Huh?"

"Hurry up."

"Ten-four."

જી

Buford Parker's coma lasted for thirteen days. Dr. Benson did not believe he would make it and told Muenter to initiate the hospital's anti-lawsuit initiative, which involved documenting power failures, contamination problems, medication shortfalls, and a list of other catastrophes, none of which actually happened. Muenter had his own list of protocols to fend off unjustified actions against him, and he mobilized to get them all into place.

On the sixth day Benson fully expected the patient to expire and put in a call to Tranchini at Brackenridge. Tranchini immediately canceled his rounds and went over to State to see Parker. "What exactly was your diagnosis of this man?" Benson asked him. "In all my years of practice I've never seen anyone with this array of symptoms."

"We never did figure out what happened to him, but we thought we'd pulled him through. He looks ten times worse than when we released him."

Benson knew that Tranchini was right and went into lawsuit-protection-mode. "We had a perfect storm of events here that easily could have killed everyone in the place – a three-hour power outage, a plumbing disaster that flooded the kitchen and a disease breakout that is still affecting half the patients."

"I'm going to have him transferred back over to my unit at Brackenridge."

"'Fraid we can't let you do that. He's ours."

"Yours! You're killing him. He needs medical care, not psychiatric care. If we cure him you can have him back."

"He stays here."

Tranchini left, disgusted. He never again saw Parker or Benson. Six months later he was admitted to a plastic surgery residency in Torrance, California, and two years after that he was taking the hooks and crooks out of three to four noses per day.

Meanwhile on the thirteenth day at Austin State, Buford Parker emerged from a coma for the second time in two weeks. On this occasion it was different. He had infections from head to toe. His blood pressure was critically low, and it took every ounce of his strength to move – even to adjust his position in bed. He lay on his back for three weeks, having to be fed and cared for by the staff at State. While barely able to move, he was not unable to think.

Three weeks after he emerged from his coma he was able to sit up in bed and eat from a hospital table pulled in front of him. His cuts began to heal and most of the infections disappeared as a result of a menu of several antibiotics and heavy doses of electrolytes. Slowly he regained his strength, knowing that any behavior that could be interpreted as hostile or even irregular would be his ticket to the tank. So he behaved angelically. In the infirmary neither Doowite nor Vinnie had much to do with him, which was okay with Buford except that he still wanted to buddy up with Doowite.

But he charmed the nurses with lies about his life and about their beauty, and before long he was riding around both floors of the hospital in a wheelchair pushed by one of the nurses. His senses were alert to every entry, every exit, and every window. He also kept track of deliveries and garbage service as well as the comings and goings of staff. By the end of the year, other than atrophied muscles, he was at full strength but kept that to himself. The wheelchair tours continued. He brain-filed every piece of information that would get him out of there. He charmed the nurses, especially Polly the wheelchair nurse. He made up a song that began, "Polly, oh Polly, dear sweet Polly, Will you, oh will you be my dolly?" Polly was as cute as her name, and she grew very fond of Buford, who she called Boof.

CHAPTER TWO

Santos, Brazil was the home of Pele the great Brazilian soccer player, and one trip up Mount Serrat, a shrine adorned hill at the harbor entrance, would confirm the popularity of the sport in that part of the world. Two dozen or more soccer fields could be seen from the summit, an hour or several hour walk from the base, depending on the pace,. Ricardo "Richard" Wilson had made the trek many times, sometimes alone and sometimes with his wife, Ingrid. Ingrid had lived in the seaport city as a young woman, and after much coaxing had convinced Richard that they should go there to live. They got married in the huge cathedral in the middle of the city and during the following year had constructed a fabulous beach house on a long white strand several miles north of the harbor entrance.

Rico and Ingrid were as passionate about each other as the day they met in Paita, Peru. Their life was now simple. Richard caught warm water marine fish with a spear or on a line from a twenty-foot dory he built well before the house was finished. Most were grilled over mesquite charcoal, occasionally accompanied by feijoada, a roasted vegetable mixture, or by home grown lettuce and tomato salad. Many evenings were spent sipping Cachaça, a rum-like drink with a long Portuguese history. They chatted in Portuguese, Ingrid's native tongue, which Richard, already fluent in Spanish, had picked up very quickly.

13

This southern hemisphere winter evening was accompanied by a warm breeze, and Rico and Ingrid were on the veranda enjoying their favorite drink. For a month or more Richard had been unsuccessful in quelling a desire to take a flyfishing vacation. He was a happy man in his new life, but it was not at all like the adventure he came to cherish guiding flyfishing tours in Argentina.

"Maybe we should go to Tandil and see if my camp on the Riachuelo Gato is still there. You've never even been there, my love."

"Ha! Maybe you could meet your old buddy Buford there. You could trap some Pampas cats while you were at it."

Richard noted a faint note of sarcasm in the response. This from a woman who was seldom anything other than aboveboard in her interactions. "We could afford it," he said.

"Rico, I'm sorry. I don't want to go back there. There are many happy memories, yes. But too many sad ones. Stressful ones. We should let them stay in our memories where they now reside. A memory can be brought to consciousness in any form or at any time that you want it. That's what makes them such a treasure."

Richard had pondered the idea too long to be put off so quickly. In fact, he did not know where he was headed with the subject because even though he loved flyfishing, he had a newfound pleasure in catching the fish species that were so abundant a stone's throw from their house. "I wonder what ever happened to that scoundrel, Parker?" he pondered out loud without looking up at Ingrid.

"I don't. That is something that we don't need to know."

"You're probably right." Rico put down his drink and walked out to the mahogany rail of his long veranda, gazing at the moonlight sparkling on the ocean surface. He and Ingrid had left Buenos Aires on a dilapidated freighter that carried cattle bones to Brazil and returned with coffee beans. Ingrid cooked for the small crew, and Richard painted the rust-flaked superstructure with thick tar-like paint. The bunks they were given were separated by a bulkhead, and one night Richard heard a muffled scream from Ingrid's side. He quietly opened the hatch and found a small Argentine named Baltisario Rana being fended off by Ingrid. Richard quickly overpowered the little man and threw him overboard. Rana's absence was not discovered until the next day. The captain of the little merchant ship only said, "I wonder if he can swim. One would hope so with a name like Rana."

Richard gazed out at the dark sea, seeing the occasional glow of bioluminescence in the surf. He had crafted their beautiful home out of local materials, rustic yet elegant, and felt a glow of pride and contentment about his life. Yet it was not by accident that Buford Parker had invaded his thoughts. Richard occasionally had dreams of the roly-poly man. Richard and his two female accomplices had left Parker tied to a tree where they had poured Pampas cat pheromones on him. One would have thought that would be the end of him, but Richard knew that it wasn't.

At that time the Coast Guard and FBI were not only looking for Richard, but had been getting very close. He also suspected that even now, the investigation was still alive within the Coast Guard, if not all of the federal investigative agencies. But before he and Ingrid had left Buenos Aires he had received a letter from Karole Kaye. How she had got the information she didn't say, but she knew that the Coast Guard had found Buford before he died and had taken him to a hospital in Austin. That's all Karole knew, at least at the time she wrote, and that was all that Richard knew. Richard had, on occasion, considered writing to Karole to tell her where he and Ingrid were living, but the dangers were too great. Nobody knew where they were and it needed to stay that way. Karole had made it clear without any subtleties that she was in love with Richard. He smiled at this thought, remembering her several proposals and that when they went their separate ways she still had one of the magic testicles in a vial of vodka. *I wonder if she still has it?* he mused.

He turned to look at his beautiful wife sipping her Cachaça, the thought of their many adventures together causing him to smile. Ingrid saw the twinkle in his eye. "What are you thinking, Riquito?"

"Nothing."

"One does not smile when they think of nothing."

"I was thinking about our adventurous life."

"It has been good. It was our rare good fortune to meet. How I remember that lovely evening in the hotel bar in Paita. How long ago was it? Five, six years?"

"Yeah, six, I think."

"Come back to your chair and tell me why you would want to leave this perfect place to visit your old camp on the Riachuelo. Is the draw of flyfishing really that strong?"

"Yeah, no. Not really, I guess. God, I did love it. That place was amazing. But no, that's not what's really pulling at me."

"Something is. I know you too well, darling. You might as well tell me."

Richard knew she was right. Even the first night at the hotel in Paita she knew that he was not telling her the truth. It was as if she could hear his unspoken thoughts. "Well, my dear, the truth is I want to find out what ever happened to that fiend, Buford. There are certain people who do our wonderful world a disservice, and Buford Parker is one of them. It runs in the family, I guess. Did I ever tell you that his great grandfather was a notorious outlaw? They made a movie about him."

"Well, that is quite a surprise. I thought we had forgotten about Mr. Parker."

"We hadn't. You had, maybe, but I hadn't."

"What makes you think going to your camp would help you find Buford?"

"I don't. In fact I know he's in Austin, Texas – or at least he was a couple years ago. God, I would like to wet a fly in the Rio Pantera. What a trout stream."

"Riquito, your signals are getting crossed. Do you want to fish or find Parker?"

"Both. I guess what I really want to do is find Parker."

"And if you were to find him?"

"I have killed once. I could do it again."

"You killed a man to protect me. To chase after Parker and kill him would be premeditated murder. That would be foolish"

"Most of my life has been foolish."

"Not premeditated murder foolish."

"My dear, foolish is foolish. There are no degrees of foolish. Foolish is what it is. Just foolish.

"If you really must find Parker, I need to go with you."

"Why do you say that?"

"Safety. I am careful. You are careless – and foolish."

"Darling, I am going to look for Parker. You will stay here. I don't really intend to kill him, but I need to know his fate – what ever happened to that piece of shit. But you know, darling, I do need to do something to that man that will help him remember me. He stiffed me for bookoo bucks – one million Abes to be exact."

"Forget it Ricardo. Parker is worth less thought than that green lacewing on the sleeve of your white shirt."

Richard looked at the fragile creature on his sleeve. "I am going. Not tomorrow, but within the month. You will be safe here until I return. And of course I will stay in touch."

Ingrid had never seen Richard so adamant and assured about anything. She could see that he would have his way no matter what she said. Even in full awareness of that, she said, "Please don't. It is too dangerous. If you go to the United States you will be caught and they will lock you up and throw the key into the ocean."

"I have to. I have a friend who I think lives in Austin, Texas. I don't know for sure, but there is a good chance that he's still there. I can hide out at his place."

"Who is it? You never mentioned any friend there."

17

"His name is Willy. Willy Lopez. We went to grade school together in Mexico. The last I heard he was working in Austin. My suspicion would be that it is not a conventional type of job, but I'll find that out when I get there."

"And what do you mean by conventional job?"

"Willy tends to operate in ways that might not always be in conformance with the law. He is very clever. I suspect he will be able to help me accomplish my mission."

"You have a mission?"

"Yes. Maybe I don't now. But by the time I reach Austin, I will know what it is."

CHAPTER THREE

Paula Burris, nee Paul Burton, knew she had to call Karole Kaye. It had been two weeks now and she had punched in Karole's number several times, but had stopped the call even before the ringing started. Paula was not shy. But as a transsexual who kept her sex reassignment a secret, she had, perhaps, an exaggerated idea of privacy and the invasion of anyone's "space," as she thought of it. Nevertheless, she knew this call had to be made and it was with resolve on Saturday at around ten-thirty that she punched in Karole's number for the severalth time. The seven rings seemed like an eternity to her, but she did not buckle. When Karole answered, Paula said, "This is Paula. Is this a bad time?"

"Paula! Bad time? Paula, there's no bad time. My god, Paula I can't believe I'm talking to one of my all time heroes."

"Oh god, Karole, I was worried you wouldn't even remember who I was."

"Get outa here. You are the most amazing person I've ever met. Are you still in Omaha?"

"Yeah, still *live* here, but I'm on the road most of the time."

"Well get on the road and come over here. I'm in Ames now. You could get here in three hours or less. I'll make dinner for you and you can spend the night."

"I sure don't want to bother you and your husband, Karole."

"Uh, you won't bother me, and I don't have a husband, pal. How come you're on the road a lot?"

"I travel for my work. I can't believe you're not married. You're so beautiful."

"Okay, what's your work? My god, Paula, getting anything out of you is like trying to pluck a feather from a flying bird."

"I just didn't want to take up your time."

"Come on. I just invited you to come over. Can you do that?"

"Sure, it sounds like fun. Anyway, there's something I want to tell you. You might know it already, but if you don't, it will be exciting for you."

"Wow, now that's something to look forward to. I've been meaning to call you. I mean, sure that's a little hard to believe after, what, two years? But I have a photograph of you that is probably the best picture ever taken."

"What is it? What am I doing?"

"Well, that'll be my surprise to you."

"What shall I bring?"

"Nothing. No. See if you can get a bottle of Malbec. We'll relive part of our time together."

"You got it, babe. I'll see you tomorrow."

"Not tomorrow. Now. I have to go to work on Monday. Come over now. Bring the wine. I'll cook us up a rib steak, just to make things authentic."

"Well, okay. If you're sure I won't be bothering you.

Paula was elated. She adored Karole. She might have hit on her if she were still Paul, but, no, Paul was gay so he wouldn't have either. She was already dressed in her usual uniform of purple and white athletic workout togs, so she grabbed her purse, fired up her new Chevy Impala and headed for Jay Vee liquors. There she found the Malbec and also grabbed some Camembert cheese and Triscuits.

The road to Ames is Interstate 80, flat, with little scenic appeal. Paula had made the trip quite a few times, and she was familiar with every tree and barn along the way. The plain tableau made the trip seem longer than it was, but by and by she found herself in Ames, at which time her Garmin road guide told her how to get to the address that Karole had given her. She arrived at three o'clock and approached the door alertly, hesitantly, but with enormous anticipation.

Karole heard her arrive and greeted her warmly. "This is a treat and a half, Paula. I can not believe that you have appeared suddenly out of the blue." Karole felt stupid for her cliché. She was a college professor after all. She could do better than that.

"I think about our adventure a lot. Especially the second one where we nailed that little shit."

"You nailed him, Paula. We just watched in disbelief. Richard kept saying, 'This is not going to work. No way. It'll never work.'"

"I knew it would. I might even tell you why if we drink enough of this wine."

"My my. The answer to a riddle is in the bottle, and I don't even know what the riddle is. First I have to ask you something that might sound rude or unfair, but I am so curious to know what made you call – I mean today, after two years?"

"Not rude, Karole. I know it's a little weird. I mean we're friends, after all. Few if any have been through some of the stuff that we did together. But, yeah, of course, there was a trigger."

"God, I can't wait. Can I get you some tea?"

"No thanks. Got any Coke Zero?"

"Nope. Sorry about that." Karole thought for a moment. It was two years old, but she had kept it in the freezer. "How about some maté?"

"Amazing. Maté would be great."

Karole lived in a nice neighborhood near the Iowa State campus. She knew and lived near Amy Toth, who was also on the faculty at Iowa State, but Karole did not know that Amy had briefly been a suspect in the Cornfield Cages murder, a gripping event described in *The Oncorhynchus Affair*. Paula and Karole settled with their drinks in a wood-paneled room heated by a Blaze King stove. "Okay, what's up?" Karole asked.

"I'm not even going to say guess what, because you couldn't guess in a million years." Paula hated drama, so her pause was scarcely noticeable. "I saw Richard."

Karole felt her skin tingle and wondered if she was blushing. "You saw him? Are you sure it was Richard? Where? Jesus. When?" Karole was disarmed. If her thought process had a censor, it suddenly disappeared. The mention of Richard's name sent her imagination into a beautiful chaos.

"Santos. A couple weeks ago."

"Santos. Where the fuck is Santos? Pardon my language, by the way. I tend to get a little crude when I'm excited."

"Brazil."

"Brazil. Jesus, Paula, what were you doing in Santos, Brazil?"

"It's kind of a long story."

"I don't give a shit. What do you think you're here for? Tell it. You know I'd crawl a hundred yards over razor blades just to catch a glimpse of that hunk of manhood." Karole made no effort to hide her excitement.

"I figured you'd want to know. So here's the story. I work for an advertising agency. It's a big agency and they have the Chevy account, which they gave to me. Actually they didn't give the account to me, but I fulfill a key need in the advertising program, you might say. Don't know if you noticed, but my ride is a new Impala. Chevy gives me one every year."

"I noticed. Jesus, Paula, get on with the story."

"Have you ever paid any attention to car commercials? They're all the same. They just show a new car going over some fabulous road, as if, when you buy the car, suddenly you find yourself in some fantastic place. It is so stupid. I mean think about it. What happens if you buy the car. You go to work in it on some jammed commute route and if you're lucky you have a good CD to listen to, while some asshole tries to get to work three minutes sooner by cutting in and out of the clogged lanes."

"Paula? Was one of the assholes Richard? In other words, might you be including some details in this story that I don't need to know?"

"Maybe it's the maté. This stuff has me feeling great."

"Glad to hear that, Paula," Karole said.

"You're really sweet to have me over, Karole. Okay, I know I'm stringing this out too much, but I think it's relevant. So anyway, my job is to find the fabulous roads. Can you believe it? They pay me to travel all over the world to find roads. I look for roads that are ultra-scenic and interesting, maybe with a bear or a moose or something near it. Or lots of curves, beautiful mountains. Just check out the commercials. That's all they do is drive on the road I pick, and they hope it's better than the road that the Toyota or Ford will be driving on a few minutes later on the same program. Stupid. But, hey, you should hear where I've been."

"Let me make a guess. Santos."

"Well, sort of. My destination was Rio. Rio de Janeiro. You would not believe the beauty of that city… and the road choices. You could make a year's worth of commercials right there. But, anyway… in my other life, which I might explain to you later, I was a really promising soccer player, and my idol, of course, was Pele. Santos is where Pele is from. I'm not sure, maybe he still lives there. I know he's had a heap of health problems, so he probably moved. So, anyway, as long as I was in Brazil, I decided to go up to Santos and see if I could see Pele. Not really see him, but look at the commemorative stuff that was sure to be around – and was, by the way. It was just fantastic to see all the stuff in the museum there.

"I rented a Chevy, and of course there are some fabulous roads along the route to Santos. Anyway, Santos is a sea port about six or so hours south of Rio, and right at the entrance to the harbor is a big hill. It's called Mt. Serrat. It has a road to the top that would make a pretty good Chevy commercial, but it's foot traffic only. So here's the meat. The rest of the story has been bun, you might say, so here's the meat. I trekked up the road to the top of Serrat, and spy Richard sitting on a bench in front of a shrine."

"My god, did he remember you?"

"Karole, I chickened out. I just watched him for awhile and then left him there. It was a private moment for him, and I didn't want to invade."

"Oh, dear god. This is too much. You didn't even say, 'Hey'?"

"No, I'm sorry, Karole. I feel like a fool, but yep, I'm a chicken."

"That's okay, hon. It took a fair amount of guts to tell me the story, given the ending."

"I know. I know. But we know where he is. Isn't that worth something?"

"Of course it is, Paula. Of course it is. What about Ingrid? Was she with him?"

"Nope. I never met Ingrid. But Richard was alone."

The maté sipper that Karole had given to Paula was, as are almost all sippers, made from a gourd. This one had intricate paintings on it and sterling silver adornments. The straw was silver with a strainer at the base to keep the maté leaves from entering the straw. During their last trip to Argentina, Paula had come to like the bitter drink, but unlike Karole she had not brought any of the tea nor the sipper back with her. "I wish I'd brought a sipper back with me," she said. "I love this stuff."

"I bet you can get one online. My god, you can get whatever you want on line. I'm guessing you'd like a refill."

"For sure. Thanks."

When Karole returned, she wanted to glean more information about the Richard Wilson sighting, but couldn't think up a good question. Finally she said, "Was he praying?"

"Who?"

"Who? Who are we talking about?"

"Oh, yeah. Richard. No, I'm pretty sure he was just sitting there. Maybe resting. It's a strenuous climb. You know, Karole, I hardly ever talk to people. You'll have to forgive me if I get lost sometimes."

"Don't worry. Anything else come to mind about the RW sighting?"

"No. Nope, just what I told you."

"I'm glad you did. He found his way out of Argentina. That's good. I wonder if the Coast Guard is still looking for him. Or the FBI. I bet they all are. Stealing a C-130 is not the same as taking a stapler from the office supply cabinet, or even, say, an outboard motor. They won't forget Richard Wilson any time soon, I'm sure."

"You were going to show me a picture."

"I took over a hundred pictures between our two trips. About half of them are of Richard. There are a few of the cats, there's even one of Buford; but, by far, the best one is of you. I picked out the best 40 or so to show you. Want to see that one first? Or should I show them in order?"

"I dunno. Why don't we start with the good one."

Karole inserted a card into the side of her TV set and selected the input. There on the wide screen was a shot of Paula unloading her bolo punch on Buford Parker. It was a thing of beauty, Parker's head snapped back, his eyes glassy. Beads of flying sweat were even visible. Both were dressed in flyfishing outfits – waders, vests, creels – the whole marianne. The two women looked at it in silent awe for awhile and by and by Karole asked the question that needed answering. "Where did you learn how to do that?"

"It's a long story."

"It really doesn't have to be, Paula. Maybe there are some details that you can leave out."

Paula took it as a slight but sure insult. "Should I leave out the part where I used to be a guy?" she asked in a way that was telling.

Karole had been holding her teacup in her hand and it started rattling on the saucer. She put them on the coffee table. "You'd better tell it your own way."

"I used to be Paul. I was so good at basketball that even in middle school people saw me going to the NBA. Then I broke my leg and it never healed right, so I couldn't play b-ball anymore, but I could box. I won the lightweight golden gloves title in Lincoln – that's where we lived. I also had a soccer scholarship offer to a couple universities. But all the while, I knew that I was a woman trapped in a man's body. I know you hear that from trannies all the time, and it's probably hard to understand if you have never been there, but that's the best way to say it. Anyway, when I was boxing I got some sixteen millimeter movies of Kid Gavilan. He used to use that punch and I worked on it until I'd mastered it – the bolo punch. If you master the bolo punch, you never forget it – even if they make you into a girl."

"Oh my god, I remember you said some vague thing that I didn't understand. Wow, Paula, I can't believe it. You were a guy? My god."

"Yep. There's actually quite a few of us around."

"Do many people know?"

"Three."

"Counting me?"

"Yep. You, my mother, and my best friend, Bob."

"Bob? Anyone I know?"

"Nope. Bob Weaver. My dad knew, but he's dead."

"Wow. Good story. Tersely told, I might add. So Bob's middle initial is N, right?"

"Good one Karole. I nailed him with a bolo punch. Down for the count, baby."

"Is Bob real?"

"Yes, I did whip him in the golden gloves, but he's not really my best friend. You are."

"Me? You can't be serious. We've spent so little time together."

"Karole, it's not the amount of time, but what happens during the time. Every minute – every second of life is a miracle – an extraordinary wondrous moment. Think of the things we did together and what we went through, just because we went to the same flyfishing class. Unbelievable, really. Think of life itself, Karole, it's so fragile. Tragedy is always lurking around the corner. So is triumph. And in the end, what is there? Death for all. These are the things that support religion. I make it sound gloomy, but life is so very beautiful. It sounds cliché to say anything about such a miraculous thing, but look around us. Look at our planet, and us, humankind, of course, but I really mean you and me specifically, we are beyond special. From the moment you and I met I saw a quality I've never known in anyone. Yes, Karole, you are my best friend. You don't need to say anything, and you don't need to worry about coming through for me in any way. You already have."

Karole was visibly moved, and clearly flummoxed. Paula knew, and could easily see, that she was laying a pretty heavy load on Karole, a woman who had been scarcely more than an acquaintance, and she watched as Karole unconsciously shifted slightly in her chair. Paula could have said more, but she knew she had said enough. Good or bad, she had said enough.

"If only Richard could say that," Karole said after a long silence. "If only Richard could see whatever it is you see."

"He does. When we were with him, he was under the spell of Ingrid. Maybe he still is, but when I saw him he was alone. He was at a shrine on Mt. Serrat. Think back to when we were setting Parker up. His admiration for you was so evident that you probably didn't even see it. You were so disappointed that he wouldn't get in bed with you that you missed the love and respect that he was keeping at bay – that he was fighting against. I'll leave it there. But it's true."

Paula had been a phenomenal athlete as a male, but knew beyond any doubt that that boy's body was meant for someone else. Now she lived in the body she should have been born with, but bore an emotional handicap that went with such a radical change in her life. Never, since she had become Paula, had she spoken from her heart. She felt good, maybe better than she ever had, but she knew it was time to stop. "What's for dinner?" she asked.

"Rib eye steaks a la Richard. Remember the last supper at his camp? With the wine you brought, of course."

"Maybe it's time to pull the cork."

CHAPTER FOUR

Although it had been two years since she had seen or heard anything about Buford Parker, Nurse Practitioner Tina Chevaria was still haunted by his last moments in the hospital ward. He had promised the most unforgettable evening of her life and it was going to be enabled by cat balls. That's how she remembered it anyhow.

As Tina, almost unconsciously, recalled the bizarre moment, an involuntary shiver caused her to spill coffee into her lap. The seemingly senseless words were Parker's last before two orderlies entered the hospital room, put him in a straitjacket and escorted him to who knows where. At the time Tina didn't know and had made the decision that she didn't want to know. Nevertheless, she had mentally replayed the bizarre scene dozens of times since, like somebody reading and rereading a paradoxical puzzle. What in the hell was the crazy loon talking about? He had been in a coma for a week, and within minutes of coming out, said that? Weird!

More mysterious was that less than a week before that happened, Tina had met her old Texas Tech roommate, Betty Jane Griffin at the Hookem House in Austin and told her about the peculiar patient, his scratch-covered body presenting symptoms so strange that no doctor in the hospital would even speculate an origin. And then, to her surprise, Betty Jane took a guess at who the guy was, and she nailed it. Of all the people in the world who this guy might be, Betty Jane correctly guessed who this crazy fat man was. Betty Jane had told her that she'd done some research for him. The two women were on their second margarita when BJ guessed Parker's name, and within a few seconds of discovering the unlikely connection, Betty Jane had bolted. Tina never could figure out why that happened, but it intensified the mystery like a clue in a whodunit that was meant to throw off the reader. *My god, has it already been two years?* Tina mused. *I've gotta move on!* Tina had, indeed, gotten to know the "friendly doctor," but she discovered that she was not alone in that regard, and he married the other. Last she heard they lived in Hollywood, where Dr. Tranchini was making a fortune doing nose jobs on movie hopefuls.

Coincidences defy logic, so maybe it should have been predictable that when Tina's phone rang it was Betty Jane. Betty Jane just said, "Hey," and Tina knew immediately who it was.

"Okay, BJ, what hole have you been hiding in?

"God, I'm sorry, Tina. Our meeting at the Hookem should have re-started a great friendship, but when you told me that you were caring for Buford Parker it kindled a memory that I didn't want to spend any time... what I mean is I was trying to forget an experience I had with him. I admit, I was curious, but not enough to find out what was up with him in the hospital and how you happened to be his nurse. It was too much. Too much."

"Okay. I sensed that. It looked like you were about to lose more than your margarita salt when you left the table. I've been about to call you a couple of times, but let's just say, it's great to hear from you, Sweetie. What's up? Getting married? Sure, I'll be a bridesmaid – no, maid of honor. Is he rich?

"Nope on all counts," Betty Jane replied, "but I would like to get together. It's been too long."

"Uh, well, why not? It's been awhile. What's up anyhow?"

"I'm finally ready to talk about the patient you told me about. The one in a coma. What ever happened to that chump? From what you told me, I made an assumption that he was about to die and then did. But now I'm going to guess that that didn't happen. That I was wrong about that. Am I right?"

"Yup. You're right. You were wrong." Tina realized that even though Parker gave every reason to conclude he was bonkers, she was still curious about what his final diatribe could have meant. Evidently Betty Jane knew something that she didn't. "I'm tied up for a couple of weeks," she said, finally. "How about meeting at the Hookem a week from Saturday."

"Straight. Noon?"

"Noon."

CHAPTER FIVE

Danny Valtino, six months away from retirement, was now the Vice Ambassador to Argentina. His primary duties were schmoozing with Argentine officials and making sure that U.S. dignitaries visiting Buenos Aires were comfortably accommodated. He was still an agent of the FBI and in his new post had more time for that assignment than he did as commercial attaché. Rosa Moreno Valtino was still his loyal wife and secretary. When Danny's extension rang at around ten on Tuesday morning, it was she.

"Danny boy, you won' believe what I jus' foun' out."

"Yes I will Rosita. You always tell me the truth."

"Oh Danny you're no fun. So I tell you anyway. Richard Wilson renewed his passaporte. Can you believe?"

"How in the world do you know that?"

"Well, we're the State Department no? I jus' ask the Passaporte Bureau to flag his name and call me if his name pop up. So I get a dispatch this morning say his name pop up."

"Did it say where he was?"

"Si, it say he's in Santos. Ju know, Santos, Brazil. Danny that big Gargantua man is no so smart, don' you think?"

"I don't know Rosa, why would you say that?"

"If he's in Brazil, he should get a Brazil passaporte. Then we would never know."

"He's not a citizen of Brazil."

"No matter, Danny. Ju jus' give some guy, some forger guy some cruzeros – that's Brazil money – ju know that – and you get a passaporte. Like you say, no fuss, no – what is the other word you say?"

"Muss."

"What is muss?"

"I don't know. Just a word, I guess."

"Okay, so he ees estupid. That's all I'm going to say. So what do we do now?"

"Good question. Let me think."

৵

"Get Bart Knowland in the DC office for me please, Rosa."

"Chure, Danny."

Bart Knowland had been interviewed, and actually selected to be the FBI Director, but turned down the opportunity for "personal reasons." He was then told that he would never be promoted within the bureau if he turned down the prestigious position of Director, but he held to his better judgment and had counted his blessings more than once as the formerly-stable position now changed hands like a game of three card monte.

"Good morning, Danny. *Que tal?*"

"Good, Bart. Good. Six months to go. How are things up there in zooland?"

"Zoo-like. What's up?"

"Rosa tells me that our old friend Richard Wilson is in Santos. She had him flagged by the Passport Bureau, and he applied for a renewal. My Rosa is something else, Bart."

"She is, indeed. When was it?"

"Well she just found out. I guess it just happened."

"I'd better let the Coast Guard know. What about Wigg and Cisterna? Are they still around?"

"I'm somewhat loathe to say yes, they are."

"How's your travel budget? Maybe they could go up there and see if they can learn anything."

"International travel is a little tricky, but we might be able to arrange it. Dunno about those two guys, though. Between the two of them they're a little dimmer than Tabby. I really don't think we should use them on a mission like that."

"Who's Tabby?" Bart inquired.

"That's the dimmest star. I'm told it's getting dimmer."

"Good to know, Danny. What's the brightest one?"

"Uh, Bart, you do know that the sun is a star?"

"Oh, yeah. I forgot that one. Maybe you should go up to Santos yourself."

Danny considered the proposal. "Maybe I should," he said finally.

CHAPTER SIX

Karole pulled the cork on the Malbec and poured two glasses. She handed one to Paula and said, "There's more, just in case. It won't be Malbec, but it will be the same color." She raised her glass, "To our renewed friendship."

"I'm so relieved that you aren't dismayed by my very forward expression of admiration for you."

"My god, Paula, how could I feel anything but honored and pleased. Plus, how could I not be fascinated by your story. I mean an athlete on the edge of a very real shot at the pros, and you forgo that because you aren't the right person for the body that was going to take you there. It's not to say I understand it at all. Just that I admire you for figuring it out yourself. I wonder if Richard had any clue who he was dealing with."

"Well, nary, I'd say. I mean you told me he didn't think I could take Buford out. I cold have cold cocked that little shit with a left jab."

"You're somethin' else, Paula. So now what? You saw Richard in Brazil. I'm still in love with him. He was alone at a shrine. Am I missing anything?"

"We still don't know what happened to Buford Parker, but I think we could find out – if that seems germane."

"How could you find out?"

"Okay, when we left Buenos Aires, you flew direct to Austin. I flew to Galveston," Paula reminded her. "I figured that if I stayed there a few days I would be able to find out if the Coast Guard ever found him where we left him. I know it was a long shot, but I just wanted some 'closure,' if you'll forgive my using that stupid word. So I went to the air base in Galveston and told them that my brother had gone on an assignment in Argentina, and asked if he was back yet. The guy I talked to sent me to another guy who knew exactly what I was talking about. My biggest fear was that they would ask who my brother was."

"And they didn't. You lucked out."

"No. They did."

"Holy Christ. What did you do?"

"I said he was the skipper on the flight down to Argentina. That seemed good enough for this guy. So anyway, I stay in a motel for a couple days, and I was actually ready to give it up and leave, and on the third morning, I think it was, I get a call from Chief Somebody saying the aircraft was in if I wanted to meet my brother.

"So I go down to the airbase, and I see them escorting this guy in a wheel chair from the plane to a private vehicle. It was a Cadillac with longhorns sticking out from the front fenders. It had to be his car. Buford appeared to be catatonic. It was definitely Parker. No mistaking. I mean how could you mistake that guy? Roly poly – pink skin. It was Parker. So they put him in this car and drive away. A Coast Guard guy was driving the car – a chief petty officer, I think. So I tell another Coast Guard guy that I had thought I was supposed to carry Parker to the hospital somewhere, but he tells me other arrangements had already been made. The guy thanks me and says they're headed to Austin. I followed them up there – I mean it was no trouble following them – that car, you shoulda seen it. So anyway, the place they let him out was Brackenridge Hospital. That's a big hospital in Austin."

"Paula, do you remember calling me right after that? I was still in Omaha and you told me that you had followed Parker up to the hospital there. That's the last time we talked."

"You're right. I completely forgot I'd called you."

"I remember because I wrote a letter to Richard to tell him. Who knows if he ever got it. I sent it to Tandil.

"So we know where Richard is," Karlole continued, "and we know where Buford was. We still don't know if we want to do anything about it, but those are some things that we know. I'll be honest with you, Paula. What I would really like to do is find Richard. I know I'm dreamin' but you know me. I think he is out of this world. I still love the guy."

"Go for it, babe. You only live once. I could go along and disappear if it looked like things might work out for you."

"Foolhardy. That would be absolutely nuts, Paula. What would I say?"

"You don't have to know what you're going to say before you say it, Karole. If you get the chance, let your heart talk."

"There is one thing you don't know, my friend."

"What could that be?"

"I still have a magic morsel. Richard gave me two, and I still have one."

"Hallelujah!"

CHAPTER SEVEN

The sun twinkled in the dew drops that had settled during the night in the rose garden and on the blades of grass in front of the Austin State Hospital. After a year of good behavior, Buford was allowed to exit the hospital interior, as long as he was accompanied by staff. Still in a wheel chair, it was Polly who was always his escort.

"Do you have a sweetheart, Polly?" Buford inquired as they admired the roses.

"I did," Polly said with a Texas accent as thick as Buford's.

"Well, honey, it sounds like there's a sad story in there somewhere.

"Oh, I'm over it, I guess."

"Maybe you could tell me a little about him, honey. You know talk is good therapy. Hell, I don't need to tell you that, you're a psychiatric nurse."

"Oh, no. I'm a CNA. I don't even have an RN."

"Lordie, what in the world is a CNA?"

"Certified nursing assistant. I could get an RN in a year, and I was going to take a leave and do it, but I like my assignment here. I like pushing you around, Boof."

"Well, I sure enjoy being pushed around by you, sweetheart. Maybe you should break my heart with your sad story."

"Oh, Boof. It *is* sad. My boyfriend's name was Donny Ray. Donny Ray Fowler. Such a cute name. And he was a pretty cute guy."

"*Was*? He didn't die, I hope."

"No. He didn't die. Donny Ray works over at the Jack in the Box over by the stadium. You know the stadium where the Longhorns play football?"

"A'course, honey, I know the place. I've had m'share of jumbo jacks, right there. He cooked em up I expect."

"No, he wasn't the chef. He was the manager. He would oversee everything, from the chefs to the sales force. He had a Jack in the Box hat. He even had a seven year service pin."

"Seven years? That seems like a funny time to have a length-of-service pin. What do you suppose is up with that?"

"Well, it's just that they don't have a five-year pin, so they have a seven-year one. He started there sweepin' floors, and now he's the manager."

"Well, Gah-lee. Think of that."

"I know. I know. But Donny Ray got too big for his boots. Boof, Donny Ray started thinking that a Jack in the Box manager was too good for a CNA. He has a girlfriend now that is a beauty advisor over at Macy's."

"Beauty advisor. What's that?"

"She demos cosmetics. Donny Ray thinks that as a manager, he should have a girlfriend that has equaled his achievement at Jack in the Box. He struts around with this beauty advisor like he's some fightin' cock or somethin'."

"That'll happen on the coattails of success. Say no more."

"I didn't want to bore you, Boof. You're so sweet."

"How could you bore me? You're the prettiest and the cleverest girl in Austin, Texas. There's not a doubt in the world about that."

"Gosh, Boof. Sometimes you make the hair on the back of my neck feel like it's tickling me. You are the sweetest man I've ever met. I can't figure out what you're doin' in here."

"Honey, it's all a big mistake. Some day I'll explain it all to you."

CHAPTER EIGHT

In the two yeas since the Coast Guard had narrowly let Commander Richard Wilson slip through its fingers, Captain Sweeny had retired, and Lt. Commander Billy Joe Bunch had assumed the job. Bunch, now a full Commander, was alone in his adamancy to find and capture Wilson, who by all accounts had disappeared from the face of the earth. Bunch knew he hadn't, but his inquiries since he took over for Sweeney had all ended in failure.

Bunch was assigned to Missing Persons Branch of the Fugitive Division in DC. His usual investigations concerned search and rescue missions in which helicopters would disappear after completing a mission. Invariably, the outcome would be that weather forced deviation from the assigned landing site. These cases were always resolved in less than a day, which was part of the reason he was able to maintain his focus on the Wilson case. Wilson had taken off from San Diego in a C-130 which was later found in Antarctica. Wilson was still at large, but it had been confirmed that he had spent several years guiding small groups on flyfishing trips near Tandil, Argentina.

A Coast Guard search party that had been sent to Argentina not only failed to apprehend the fugitive, but resulted in the civilian accompanying them being clawed nearly to death by wild felines in the area. Subsequently Wilson had disappeared. Bunch had been a big fan of "The Fugitive" television series, and thought of himself as Lieutenant Gerard.

CDR Bunch had a thick file on Wilson and was reading it when his phone rang. "Billy Joe?" inquired a voice that Bunch immediately recognized, even though he hadn't spoken to him for a couple of years. "This is Bart Knowland."

"Good morning, sir."

"I called to keep you apprised of some new information we have received on Richard Wilson."

"Excellent, sir. What's the info?

"We think he's in Santos, Brazil."

"May I ask the source?"

"He applied for a US passport renewal. The passport division of State had his name flagged."

CDR Bunch felt the way he used to when he ran onto the field at Lumberjack Stadium, where he saw occasional duty as a wide receiver for Humboldt State. "If I can get approval from the admiral, I am personally going to go down to Santos and apprehend that scoundrel myself. Have you got any plans for the Bureau?"

"At the moment the plan is for me to fly down to Santos, myself. That may change. We have a guy in Argentina that may make the trip, but at the moment it looks like me."

"Good sir. Shall we coordinate the mission?"

"I'll have a code phone with me. The access number is 8248 and my own unit is 242. I should be to Santos within two weeks, so whenever you get there you can get in touch."

"Yes, sir. I will do that. Thanks for keeping me in the loop."

CHAPTER NINE

Paula said, "Hey, babe, what's in the other bottle of wine you were talking about?"

"It's a California Zin. I drink it all the time. Think it's time to get into it?"

"Well, the Malbec's gone. That should be a clue."

"You're right. This calls for a celebration. You still have to help me figure out how to capture my man. You know, if I could figure out how to contact him, I bet I could convince him to go back to his campsite on the Riachuelo Gato for a week. I could just ask him if he'd guide me. I don't know, Paula, what should I do?"

"I'm torn, Karole. To be honest, I'm more interested in finding out what happened to Buford Parker. Nothing I'd like better than to give him another one to the chops."

"This is a dilemma. Do we split up, or work as a team?"

"The info we have is on Richard. We don't have anything on Parker, unfortunately. Maybe I'm the one who's dreaming," Paula said. "But I'm thinking maybe I could get it from someone at Brackenridge."

"Dollars to donuts, there's more interesting stuff to do in Santos, than in Austin."

"I think you could be wrong, Karole. Austin has a lot going for it."

"Listen Paula, I can afford a ticket to Santos. And you can tell your company that there are some roads down there that demand some model of Chevy to be driven on them. We should do this thing together. Wouldn't you like to go back to the place where Pele grew up? Yes, you would."

"Karole, you don't even know where Richard is. Santos is huge. What are you going to do? Wait for him to show up at Mount Serrat again? That's silly. Just 'cause I saw him there doesn't mean that's where he hangs."

"He's six-four and blond. How many of those are in Santos? All we have to do is ask around."

"Ask who? What language do they speak there? I don't think it's Spanish."

"I don't care if it's Swahili. There's always someone around who can speak English. We could find him and we could have fun doing it. What do you think, Paula? If you find Buford, what have you got. Nothing. Just some bit of knowledge that is of no use. I mean really, what are you going to do? Bolo punch him? Kick him in the balls? Then what? Walk away and wait until the cops show up and arrest you for assault? You would be very unhappy in jail, Paula. Plus, right now Parker doesn't know who you are. I can't say for sure, but he strikes me as vindictive. If you get in his way, he would stalk you until he got even. Just forget about Parker and come along with me to Santos Brazil."

"I'd have to see if they're interested in more Brazilian roads. They've used a couple of the ones I chronicled for them. I must say, they loved them. Chevrolet doesn't even bother to mention that they're in Brazil."

"Now you're talking. Santos here we come. Oh, my god, Paula, what if we actually find my beefcake? What if he's dumped Ingrid? I could wind up living in Brazil. Do you suppose I should get a one-way ticket?"

"Karlole, you need to get your head straight. The likelihood of any of that happening is somewhere around zilch."

"I don't care. I'm taking my last Pampas Cat jewel along, just in case. Paula, I think there's a pretty good chance he's been thinking about me. After all, I'm not all that bad looking, and I love to fish. How could he do better than that?"

"Karole, nobody could do better than you. Just don't get your hopes up, okay? Keep in mind that the last we know he is a still a married man."

"The good news is that last we know was two years ago. For all we know he might be shoppin'."

"What?" Paula asked.

"He might just be shoppin'. You know. Shoppin'."

"I doubt that, babe, but I'll see if I can get the company to finance another trip to Brazil. If not, I'll pay my own way. Even though it costs me a fortune to be a lady, my bank account is actually in pretty good shape."

CHAPTER TEN

When Polly Kjelson knocked on Buford Parker's door Wednesday morning a voice she recognized as Wilmer Throckmorton's screamed out, "Parker ain't here."

Confused, Polly opened the door. For over a year she had followed a routine of three knocks then a pause and then one more. Buford would respond by whistling a bar – or perhaps both bars – of Polly, oh Polly, Dear sweet Polly and then softly holler, "Come right on in, Sweetheart." For at least a year, Parker could have dressed himself, but he did not let Polly know that, and he enjoyed it when she would help him on with his clothes.

Parker shared a room with Wilmer Throckmorton, who had been committed after strangling a man to death at a Longhorns football game. Just as rabid a Texas fan as Parker, Throckmorton had not taken well to an A&M fan's loud ridicule of the Longhorns during a game in which the Aggies kicked a field goal with only 23 seconds left in the game, even though they already led the Longhorns by 42 points. His clever lawyer pleaded insanity and Throckmorton got off with a commitment to Austin State Hospital. At first Parker had admired his roommate for the bold act, but truth be told, Throckmorton truly was a mental mess, and over time his constant rants about everything from contemporary art to the fools who abolished slavery got under Buford's skin. Polly hated and feared Throckmorton and so she was trepidatious as she entered the room. Even as she crossed the threshold, she could feel Throckmorton's wild eyes undressing her. As she backed out and shut the door, she could hear his maniacal laughter following her as she scurried away pushing the empty wheelchair ahead of her.

The duty nurse, Tanya Hyde, checked the discharge reports for Polly and neither the past nor coming weeks had any entry. "Could he be out in the gardens on his own?" she asked Polly.

"I don't think so. He needs my help dressing."

"And he doesn't walk, even with a walker?"

"No. No, he needs assistance getting in and out of the chair. No way could he get anywhere on his own."

"I'd better call Mr. Muenter," Tanya said in a frightened tone.

"Muenter," she heard on her end of the line.

"Mr. Muenter, Buford Parker was not in his room this morning when Polly went to pick him up."

"What do you mean by pick him up."

"Parker is on yellow flag, and Polly takes him for a turn in the garden in his wheelchair every day for a couple of hours."

"Where is he now?"

"That's what I'm trying to tell you. He appears to be missing."

"Is Doowite around?"

"Yes. I see him over with one of the patients. Mr. Hurt, I think."

"Ask him to come up to my office please, Tanya."

"Yes, sir. I'll tell him."

"What's up, Chief?" Doowite asked as he entered Muenter's office.

"Where's Parker?" Muenter replied.

"I haven't had to deal with that asshole since about the fourth week after he got here. Last time I talked to him was a couple of months ago. He was begging me for my autograph. I get five bucks a signature and he never offered me a cent."

"He might be hiding out somewhere. He wasn't in his room when one of the CNAs went there to take him out."

"Want me to organize a search?

"No."

"What do you want me to do?

"Of course I want you to organize a search. Why do you think I brought you in to tell you he was missing?"

"Ten-four, Chief. No need to get huffy. In fact it would be good to remember that even though you were a coach and I was a player, that we are both retired from those jobs. I'm seven inches taller than you and sixty-five pounds heavier. Keep in mind too, that your head is a big as a large pumpkin, and it would take a real effort to miss it. Just sayin'."

"Doowite. Get out of here."

&

Doowite and Vinnie organized a dozen off-duty employees into a search party. There was a standard protocol and it was not uncommon to find missing patients within an hour. Occasionally, patients suffering from depression were found after having committed suicide. On this occasion the search lasted for just under three hours and Parker was not found. Muenter had Throckmorton brought into his office and questioned him for a half hour. "When did you last see Parker?" he asked. Was Parker acting odd in any way? Did you ever see Parker walk on his own?"

Throckmorton, squirming around like a cerebral palsy victim, yelled between animated breaths "Fatty's missing? That little shit fooled you?" His laughter was so wildly raucous that Muenter had to have Doowite take the kicking madman back to his room.

&

Inmates at Austin State Hospital wear issued clothing. During the warmer months they wear white nylon pants with an elastic waistband and yellow nylon v-neck tops. Buford knew during his year of planning his escape that it was well known to nearly everyone in Austin that this was the uniform that the crazies in the hospital wore. Most of the employees wore uniforms as well, and in fact he had concluded that only the administrator, Robert Muenter, the physician, Jerome Benson, and the psychologist, Laura McAllister, wore civvies. Owing to disparities of gender or size, none of the three would have clothes in their lockers that would be suitable for Parker's escape.

Parker had orchestrated his escape by activating the fire alarm at eleven o'clock at night when the shifts were changing. Although twice as many people were present, the geometric increase in the confusion level enabled him to exit an unguarded rear door with an alarm switch. The door alarm was similar to the fire alarm, and nobody noticed that the two were sounding together. Subsequent to his escape, the entire night shift had been replaced by the day staff and it wasn't until well after Parker had gone missing that Muenter even saw the fire alarm report.

Now, after a precarious six hours crawling and sneaking through allies and yards, with the occasional dog signaling his presence, and emerging daylight beginning to illuminate the morning, Parker judged that he was about two miles from the facility. He was reasonably agile, but not in good shape, so his movements had to be accomplished in short bursts. The urge to run into a second hand store, or even a department store, grab some clothes and run out were overwhelming, but he knew that he would be pursued and would not be able to outrun anyone. Parker was a wealthy man, but at this moment he had not a cent, and his outfit carried not only instant ID, but the stigma that went along with being nuts. No bribes or payoffs were available to him and realizing the importance of the next couple of hours, he felt an impotence that he was not accustomed to. For most of his life, Buford Parker had called the shots one way or another, and he could not help thinking back to the horrible ordeal he had gone through two years previously – the only other time in his life when he was not in charge. The present moment – this moment without any plan – this predicament or plight – was the Achilles heel of his careful design for escape. He thought of the movie *The Great Escape* in which a magnificently conceived project began to fall apart even before the prisoners started their breakout.

His ranch was ten miles out of town. Ideally, he needed to get there, and he had to figure out how to do it before the morning unfolded in its full splendor. He thought back to four murders he had committed in a remote part of Argentina. He had felt no guilt at the time. Could he murder for a suit of clothes? It seemed unlikely to him that he could overcome anyone, even if he had a weapon of some kind. He shivered in his hiding place.

CHAPTER ELEVEN

The Hookem House is a warehouse-size bar and grill near the campus of the University of Texas. Tina hadn't seen Betty Jane since their last drink there two years ago, but in the ten years or so since they graduated from Texas Tech, they had maintained the timeless friendship that college roommates often share. Over the course of their undergraduate years they had downed their share of spirits in Lubbock, the home of Texas Tech. By coincidence, they both wound up in Austin, and they would often get together at "the House," as they usually referred to it.

From her earliest childhood, Tina had a medical profession as her goal. Betty Jane, started out in the same major as Tina, and indeed that is how they became roommates. But Betty Jane discovered a passion for research chemistry and veered away from her initial goal of becoming a physician. She was an excellent student and didn't need to spend as much time booking as most of her peers. So she frequented a bar near campus called Reds, and it was not a rarity for her to leave with some hunk from the Red Raiders athletic program. The restaurant name Reds, without an apostrophe, was probably named for the athletic teams, but if you were to ask the bartender he would always say, "It's called Reds because we specialize in red wine and red meat."

After she moved to Austin, Betty Jane discovered the House, and that is where she met Parker, who was not a hunk by any stretch of the meaning. He was fiftyish, over-weight with moist pinkish skin and thinning strawberry-blond hair. In spite of his appearance, Betty Jane found a peculiar fascination with him.

Parker apparently had a ton of money which he spent freely, and he told strange tales, possibly untrue, about finding gold in Argentina on some property owned by his great-granddaddy, Butch Cassidy, whose real name, according to Buford, was Robert LeRoy Parker. Betty Jane and Buford became occasional lovers and it wasn't long before Betty Jane found herself living in a ranch style that Buford bought for her in Tarrytown, near the Colorado River.

During their previous meeting at the Hookem House, Tina had mentioned a strange patient that she was treating at Brackenridge Hospital, and somehow Betty Jane instantly knew it was Parker that Tina was talking about. The last time Betty Jane had been with Parker she had become sicker than she had ever been. It was a story she still didn't fully understand, and she hadn't seen Parker since that night, but she decided it was time to tell it to Tina.

Betty Jane got to the House first and admired the decor which was one hundred percent Texas Longhorn. She watched a guy get tossed off a mechanical longhorn bull, finally found a table and ordered a couple of margaritas, always their go-to drink. Tina was fifteen minutes late, and by then, Betty Jane had eaten most of the hot wings she'd ordered.

"Hey, bud," Betty Jane said as they hugged. "Thanks for coming down on short notice."

"Hey, two years is too long. I've had you on my mind ever since you ran out on me. It wasn't hard to see that you suddenly got sick. Or were you mad at me? I hope not."

"No, no, no. It wasn't that at all. It was that Buford Parker came into the conversation. Remember? You were telling me about this strange admission at the hospital, and somehow I knew right away you were talking about Buford Parker." She paused, reading Tina, whose face was blank. "Here finish these hot wings."

"So that made you sick?"

"I guess." Betty Jane felt a vague wave of nausea, but it passed. "I mean, yes, no doubt about it. See, the last time I saw Buford, it was at this ranch he has. I went out there because he said he had a new batch of cat balls he wanted to share. It didn't turn out so good."

Tina shivered again remembering the last thing Parker had said before he get escorted away in a straitjacket. "Cat balls."

"Yeah. Sounds strange, I guess."

"You guess? Strange? You guess? Don't you mean fuckin' freaky. Have you ever been horny?"

"Duh."

"No, I mean, well, I doubt you'd really understand what I'm talking about unless you'd tried one. I know I had my doubts."

"One what? A cat ball. No thanks."

Betty Jane sighed. She realized that this was going to be a difficult conversation.

⅋

"Let's start by filling up our glasses. Even the abbreviated version of this story is going to take awhile." They ordered a pitcher of margos from a twenty-something year-old guy wearing a well-worn burnt orange letter sweater. He hit on them briefly, but gave up figuring they were lesbos. Betty Jane continued. "I met Parker right here about five years ago. He wound up buying me the house I live in, because I did some research for him. Research and production, actually. He had a sample of the exudate from a female Pampas cat that was in heat." Betty Jane started to lose it again, remembering Frenzy. She never knew for sure, but she was about ninety-nine percent sure that Buford had killed her beloved cat.

"So I reproduced a chemical replica of this pheromone-laden exudate and he used it to trap Pampas cats in Argentina... or actually he had someone else do the trapping. The pheromone is what they used for bait. He wanted the male

52

cats because their balls are an aphrodisiac. So, with that in mind, take a sip and recall what you told me that Buford said just before they dragged him away. Make sense now?"

"Jesus. I can't believe what I'm hearing, but, yeah. The pieces are starting to fit."

"Tina, I know this sounds like a crock, but it isn't.

"How do you know? Please don't tell me you tried it."

"No. But when I was doing the research on the pheromone, there were these three other girls who would occasionally feed Frenzy. She was the cat that Parker brought back from Argentina. Anyway, one of 'em was Trisha. She told me that Buford gave her one. He told her that it was the mushrooms on the pizza they had.

"Eeeeww."

"She told me she didn't notice anything strange about the taste. It tasted like a regular old pizza near as she could tell. But she said to say they make you horny really sells them short. I remember her asking me something like, 'You've had bum sex, right? I mean really bum sex where it's over and you feel like... uh... nothing happened?'"

Tina intervened. "Tell me about it. I'd say about half the time."

"That's what I said. So she says, 'Think of your bummest sex ever. The deal is that if you'd eaten one of Buford's magic jewels, as he called them, it would have been the best sex ever.' That's what she said. The way I see it, eating this cat testicle must somehow flood your body with every sex hormone your body can produce. Trisha said that it goes on and on. She told me that Buford passed out and she felt like she was just getting started."

Tina sipped on her margarita and licked some salt from the rim. Impulsively, she looked at the mechanical bull just as a guy was falling off. A chorus of laughter and guffaws came from the small but enthusiastic watchers. She picked up the pitcher, refilled her glass and grabbed the last hot wing from the paper-lined plastic tray. Finally she said, "When I mentioned him a couple years ago, you about lost your lunch. What was up with that?"

"Well, we were supposed to have an all-nighter. Trish convinced me that I should go for it. It was an all-nighter, all right – an all-night battle with the grim reaper. I never got the story from Parker, but I've kind of pieced it together from some of the stuff he's told me. He went on a fishing trip down in Argentina where the cats are. There was this flyfishing guide down there, and he set up the guide with all the stuff to trap the cats and he was supposed to castrate 'em and send the balls back to Buford. I know that there was some bad blood between them. Buford used to say some very disparaging things about Richard Wilson, who was the guide, and Buford's partner in this endeavor. I know for sure that he hated this guy. Buford never told me this, and he never would, but I don't think he sent the guide the money for the balls. That's just me speculating, and so is this – I think this guy sent Buford something with poison in it, or maybe he sent some other kind of balls or something, I just don't know."

"What happened?"

"So on the night I was finally going to experience the fruits of my labor, I remembered what Trisha had said about Parker passing out before she had had enough, so I made sure that Buford had one as well. We put the magnificent morsels on the pizza, gobbled it up with great anticipation – I mean I'm sitting there in my underwear eating what I thought were Pampas cat testicles, and all of a sudden I was sicker than I've ever been in my life. So was he, Tina. I think we were both close to death. I get a little nauseated just thinking about it. God, it was awful. Since Buford ate one himself, I'm guessing that whatever it was that almost killed us was not something he had planned on. Nevertheless, some measure of retribution seems appropriate, wouldn't you think?"

"How can you say this guy is an enigma? He sounds like a pure jerk. He *is* a jerk. I had him on my floor in the hospital.

Probably the most disgusting patient I've ever had to deal with."

"He bought me a house. That probably biases my opinion some. I dunno, Tina, the more I got to know him, the more evil I saw, but he was so pathetic. You saw him. There is nothing about him that is attractive, so I guess I pitied him a little. But you are absolutely right, I should hate him. It's my underdog mentality, I think."

"He's no underdog. You should have heard him. In the fifteen minutes he was conscious, he acted like we ought to be worshiping him."

Betty Jane again thought of Frenzy, the Pampas cat that she had grown to love. A wild creature that showed affection for Betty Jane as long as Buford was not around. Frenzy would growl and hiss at Buford as if she were a tiger. She hated the man. *He did kill that magnificent beast,* Betty Jane mused. *He must have. She was in perfect health.* Suddenly she felt full of hostility toward her former lover and benefactor.

Still remembering those fifteen or so minutes after Parker had come out of his coma, Tina watched Betty Jane intently. She saw Betty Jane's face cloud, and she knew as clearly as if Betty Jane had said it that Betty Jane could see the real Buford Parker. "He killed your cat," she said softly. "He almost killed you. Did he ever apologize? I don't even need to ask."

"No. All he did was rage on about the son-of-a-bitch that sent him a 'new batch.' I remember now. He was supposed to call me as soon as he got the shipment from Argentina. I knew right then that he hadn't if he was talking about different batches. No. He never apologized. He finally told me that he'd given one to his masseuse. He just said something like, 'Well I got sick, too,' as if that made everything all right. You are right, Tina. The man finds evilness so easy to come by that it is doubly outrageous. He has no concience."

"Still want to try and find him?"

Betty Jane reviewed their conversation. "I'd like to get back at that little fat man, but I don't know exactly what I want to do to him."

"I'll be right back," Tina said, getting up from the table. She walked to a machine, filled a bowl with popcorn and returned. She stood and watched the mechanical bull for a few seconds feeling a little scorn for the riders. She returned to the table, and contemplatively, took some kernels from the bowl and ate them one by one. She pushed the bowl toward Betty Jane who still looked troubled. Finally, Tina said, "Maybe we should see if we can find that blubbery mutant. Listen, we don't even know what happened to him before he showed up at the hospital. At least we could try to find that out."

"The more I think about it, the surer I am that Parker killed Frenzy. If I see that scoundrel, there's no telling what I might do to him."

CHAPTER TWELVE

The Monday following Paula's visit, Karole had returned home after teaching her three o'clock Intro to Ecology course and poured a glass of Malbec, when her phone rang.

"This is Rico Wilson," said the caller. Karole recognized the voice instantly and dropped her wine glass. Aware that she was very close to fainting, she quickly sat in the chair by the table where her phone had been charging.

"Richard, oh my dear Richard. Paula and I were just talking about you yesterday. She saw you, Richard. She saw you in Santos."

"That's where I live now. My god, I hope she didn't tell anyone."

"Paula wouldn't tell anyone if she saw Elvis. She's got a thing about privacy."

"I kind of remember that now."

"Why are you calling? Where are you? What about Ingrid?"

"I'm in Santos. I'm still married, and I'm calling to find out if you know anything about what ever happened to Buford Parker."

"No. We don't know. Paula wants to look for him. We were talking about that just yesterday. This is amazing. I hate to admit this, but I convinced her that it would be better to look for you than to look for Parker."

"Why would you want to do that?"

"Duh. Because I'm still in love with you, stupid."

"Karole, I know you said that before, but I'm not available. I'm a married man, and I'm happy with my life."

"No you're not. If you were that happy, you wouldn't be phoning me."

"I just want to find Parker. I thought you might know where he was."

"Well, I don't. But maybe I can find out. How can I call you back?"

"I don't want Ingrid to know I'm talking to you. I'll call you in a few days. Let's say a week from today. Next Monday about the same time."

"Can't we talk a little while now?"

"No."

"Oh, my dear man. I'll look forward to next Monday."

"We're just going to discuss Parker. That's all."

"Oh, I know. That's okay."

ଔ

Paula was so doubtful that her ad agency would let her go down to Brazil again that she was very reluctant to ask. The Monday following her visit with Karole in Ames, she thought about the request all day long and even visited her boss, Jack Sears. Jack was a good guy, but when Paula sat down in the chair beside his desk, she realized that his answer would be no for sure. Thinking quickly, she asked him how his son was doing. That turned out to be worse than requesting the trip to Santos because Jack's son had been arrested over the weekend for mooning a young woman who happened to be an off-duty cop on the Omaha police force. Jack had had to post $600 for his son's bail and hire an attorney to defend him. Paula lamely offered to help in any way she could, even knowing that it was a situation in which help could only come from legal representation.

So Tuesday morning when the phone rang and it was Karole, Paula fully expected to get scolded by her dear friend who expected her to arrange a trip to Santos, but who had no understanding of the complexities of Paula's mind. When Karole gave her the details of the call, Paula was not only relieved not to get chewed out, but excited because the search was going to be for the guy she wanted to find.

"Well, my ad company wasn't going to pay my way to Santos anyway. So now what do we do?"

"We have to figure out what happened to Parker, that's what."

"How are we going to do that?"

"Paula, you're the smart one. You tell me."

"Well, truth be told, it shouldn't be too hard. After all, I know that they took him to Brackenridge Hospital. I can probably get some time off and go down to Austin. Maybe you should come along."

"I can't just take off on a moment's notice. I wouldn't be able to go until the end of summer session."

"I think I can get away. My boss likes me, even though I put my foot in my mouth at work today."

"You're such a sweetheart, Paula. Will you do that?"

"Of course. That's what I wanted to do all along."

"Okay, Paula. Keep me posted. Dreamboat is going to call me in exactly a week."

"Did he say what he had in mind if you can locate him?"

"No. He really just wanted to hear my voice, I think."

"Dream on, Honey. But don't fret. I'll let you know as soon as I find out anything."

CHAPTER THIRTEEN

As dawn emerged Buford felt near death. His nylon hospital uniform had become wet in his damp surroundings, and the breeze chilled him unmercifully as the dampness evaporated. Soon the day would warm up, but his need now was to lose the uniform that targeted him as a loony bin escapee. He was some fifteen blocks from an urban neighborhood but less than a block from one of the Red Line stations of the Capital MetroRail. No money. What to do?

As the sun rose higher and people began to appear on the sidewalks he knew he had to do something risky. The quicker he could get it done, the better off he would be. He conjured up a vision of what he needed to do. It had to involve a victim and picking that person was a key ingredient to its success. The victim should be a man; should be around his size, and should be old, or handicapped in some way. He spotted the guy after a wait of over two hours. He walked with a cane and had thick glasses. Parker was in no shape to spring from his gully and grab the guy, but he managed to clamber up the slope and overtake the slow moving old man. "Stop right there, you old piece of shit," he said quietly as he approached the man from behind. Parker stuck his finger in the guy's back and said, "Take off your coat and let it drop to the ground or I'll put a bullet through your gut. Drop the coat. Don't turn around. Just keep walking straight ahead. Don't call for help or I'll shoot you and everyone else. I'm mentally deranged."

There were others around who saw the assault in its entirety, but not a one stopped to investigate. Either they were scared, or they didn't recognize it as an attack. The old man started to say something, but thought better of it. He let the coat slide off his body and kept walking. Parker caught it as it dropped and put it on. He felt for a wallet and found one in the inside pocket. He did an about face and walked as fast as his weary legs would carry him until he came to one of the benches in the Central Park area. He took out the wallet and found forty-seven dollars. He extracted the money and left the wallet on the park bench.

Even with the coat collar turned up, he knew that he was easy to spot. The pants were unmistakable, and the yellow top was slightly visible. Nevertheless, no one seemed to be paying any attention to him. He purchased a Red Line ticket from a machine and waited less than ten minutes for the train to arrive. When he stepped out of the train less than a half hour later he was only about two miles from his ranch. *So far, so good,* he thought. *But I still need to get out to my place. How in god's name am I going to do that? I'm not even sure I can walk fifty yards, much less two miles.*

A couple of taxis were parked on the street at the station exit. Parker looked at the drivers and picked one that looked like an Afghani refugee. It took three repetitions, but he finally made the guy understand where he wanted to go. Parker looked at the meter which identified the driver as Roger Brown. *Sure.* At that moment Parker knew that he was home free. At least for now.

Parker tipped Roger Brown and waited until he had disappeared before opening the lid to his irrigation timer to access the hidden house key. The house smelled of non-use, but upon Buford's perusal everything appeared to be in order. After drinking a can of coke from the refrigerator he retired to his bedroom and fell asleep.

CHAPTER FOURTEEN

The idea came out of nowhere, and Betty Jane wondered why she hadn't thought of it before. *Because I didn't want to think about Buford Parker, that's why.* All that changed following her afternoon at the Hookem House with Tina. She punched up Tina's number, and when Tina answered, she said, "Tina, here's the plan."

"The plan? What plan? I didn't know we were making a plan."

"We weren't. I mean we didn't exactly have a plan, but we talked about trying to find out what happened to Parker."

"Okay, go ahead. I think I already don't like your plan, but go ahead."

"Tina, you've got to remember that I spent a lot of time out at Buford's ranch. I had my dear cat, Frenzy, out there and – excuse me while I barf – I had some intimate moments, plus the worst night of my life out there."

"So?"

"So I know where it is. We could go out there, scope it out, and if no one's around, we could find a way in and steal a jar of his huevos. I know where they were. He had some quart jars full. Only trouble is, there may be some poison ones."

"Get outa here BJ, we're not doing that."

"Yes we are. If we aren't, I am."

"Why? What's in it for us?"

"Tina, remember Parker's last words? What he said about the most unforgettable evening of your life being enabled by cat balls? Well, it was a mystery to you, but I know – at least I know from hearsay – what they do, and it's unforgettable.

Keep in mind that on the night Buford and I practically died, that he was all in on it. And I know for sure that he had done it before; so there you are."

"Betty Jane, you may be as off center as Parker himself."

"Maybe so, but I'm going to go out there and search for treasure. Hear me? Are you in or out?

Tina thought about what Betty Jane had said and after a few seconds said, "Okay. Let's go."

"Right now? You want to do it now?"

"No. I didn't mean right now," Tina answered. "I just meant let's do it. Maybe we should go out there this weekend. When did you have in mind?"

"I was actually thinking sooner, but this coming weekend works. How about we meet at the House and take it from there."

"Straight. Let's make it Sunday at noon this time.

CHAPTER FIFTEEN

When Buford Parker awoke, the clock said three-oh-five. It was light out, so he either slept for six hours or thirty hours. His cell phone confirmed that it had been thirty. His refrigerator had some things in it that looked as if they had once been food, but now were no doubt living ecosystems consisting of organisms that had yet to be discovered. Parker slammed the door against a reek that shot through the kitchen and hung there like something that would please a vulture.

Parker's first call was to the pizza parlor and his second was to Sears to order a new fridge.

"You'll take the old one with you?" he asked.

"Twenty dollar disposal charge," was the answer.

"Bring it out today if you can," he said. *Those scumbags would probably want a couple thou for their disposal fee if they could see what they were disposing.*

He was famished and called up an order of three combo pizzas and a sixer of Lone Star. When they arrived he devoured four of the beers and one and a half pizzas in less than and hour.

Even as he was on the phone to the parlor, the idea spawned. This man had been in an asylum for two years and had not had sex. There was a good chance that Polly might have welcomed a secret tryst, but there were cameras all over that zoo where he'd spent his previous two years, and besides, he had to keep up the appearance of being disabled. A key part of his escape plan was to appear incapable of getting around without assistance.

When he opened the pantry door to check on his stash, to his delight all was as he had left it. There were still six quart jars filled to the top with Pampas Cat testicles. Or at least three, he knew, had the real thing. One, he knew did not, and he suspected that there were two more that did not. He knew that the ones that did not, were nearly lethal. One of the jars had a sticky label on it that said *GOOD*.

Oh lordy lordy, he thought, *that little Polly would go off like a fourth of July skyrocket. Hot damn, wouldn't that be sweeter'n a pecan pie with maple sauce. Damn, she would explode. Why the girl would probably tear me apart. Oh well, good way to get torn. Oh, oh, oh. But what'll I tell her. Those fools are probably still looking for me over there. Not to worry, I'll figger sompem out.*

ꙮ

"Polly Kjelson, line one," came the call over the loudspeaker system.

Could that be Donny Ray Fowler? she thought as she scurried to her office phone.

CHAPTER SIXTEEN

Rosa's office was less that twenty feet from Danny's, but rather than talk to her in person, he always dialed her on the intercom so that the other stenos in the front office would not be distracted. "Rosa, honey," he said, "can you find out from our attache in Santos if Richard Wilson applied for an Argentine visa."

"Chure, Danny. I'll call State in Washington. That's who know what's going on."

An hour and a half later, Rosa dialed Danny's extension. "No, he dint, Danny, only a Brazil visa. Danny, if he only wants a Brazil visa, it have to mean he needs it to get back to where he came from, but where from. That's where he is now, *verdad*?"

"It sounds like he's going to the US. Where else could he go without a visa. He'd be taking a chance. Maybe I should go look for him up there."

"I need to go with you, Danny boy."

"Nope. We'd never be able to pull that off, Sweetheart. Get Knowland on the phone for me."

After a few minutes Rosa chirped, "Mr. Knowland on line one, Danny boy. He such a sweet man. He tell me to take care of you. I tell him, of course I will."

Danny smiled to himself. "You're the sweet one, Rosy." He punched in line one. "Hi Bart."

"What's up? Dan?"

"I asked Rosa if she could find out if Wilson had applied for any visas, and she found out that he only got a Brazil visa – no Argentine visa."

"Surprise, surprise. What do you think he has in mind?"

"That's the mystery at hand. My take is that he is going to the States and needs a visa to get back to Santos. It doesn't make much sense, but we know that the guy is impulsive, and I can't think of any other explanation."

"If he comes up to the US. Where do you figure he'll go?

"I should have puzzled that one out before I called. Do we have any idea what ever happened to Buford Parker?"

"We could probably get a lead from the Coast Guard," Knowland replied. "Didn't they take him out of Argentina to Galveston?"

"I think that's right. We just missed Wilson, I'm embarrassed to say. That rascal slipped right through our fingers. But yeah, you're right. The Coasties flew Parker out in one of their C-130s. Apparently they still had one left after Wilson requisitioned one for his own personal use."

"I'll put one of my guys on it," Knowland said. "We need to find out where they took Parker. My thinking is that Wilson is going after that guy. Why else would he risk setting foot back in this country?"

"I expect you're right. If you are, we can use Parker as bait, and when Wilson shows up, we set the hook. Listen, Bart, if you need a hand I'd love a little sojourn to the homeland."

"I think we'd better handle it from up here, at least for starters, Danny, but I'll keep you in mind."

CHAPTER SEVENTEEN

During the week following Richard's phone call, Karole had trouble focusing on her teaching. She was convinced that Richard's true reason for calling her was that he finally realized that it was she and not Ingrid to whom he should cast his heart.

When her telephone rang on Friday, she jumped to the conclusion that it would be Richard. *For some reason he had to call early,* she surmised as she answered.

"Hi, Babe, it's Paula," came the voice.

"Oh my god. Hey. What's up?"

"Karole, you sound like you just got TKO'd by an unranked amateur. What's the matter?"

"Nothing, nothing, Let's see, I just thought, um – well, I entered this contest and I thought you might be the judge and that I'd won. Uh, no. Not really. I don't know, just melancholy, I guess."

"You thought it was Richard."

"The caller ID said, 'unknown.' So, yeah, you're right. I did that. I guess I hoped that."

"It said unknown because I have an unlisted number, Babe. Anyway, it's me. Sorry to disappoint."

"No worries. So what have you found out?"

"Okay, I'm still in Austin. I tracked Parker to the big hospital here, Brackenridge. So I go there to see if anyone remembered the guy, and there's this nurse there that is on the same mission."

"What do you mean?"

"She and her friend are looking for Parker, too."

"Why?"

"The woman is the nurse who took care of Parker when he was in the hospital. The friend is the woman who figured out how to make the pheromone that they used to catch the cats. They're going to go out to Parker's place and try to sneak in and get some of the balls."

Karole could not believe what she was hearing. "You can't be serious. What did you tell her?"

"I told her that I had gone on a fishing trip with Wilson. I also told her that Wilson was looking for Parker."

"Paula, do really think that Richard wants to find Parker? I think he wants to hook up with me. The Parker story is just a line to get with me."

"Think what you wish, Karole, but I'm sorry to have to inform you that you're head is in the clouds this time. I have never in my life seen anyone so devoted to a spouse."

"Then why would he call me?"

"Karole, he is looking for Parker. He hoped you might know something, and now you do."

"Did they know where Parker is?"

"No. The nurse told me that they hauled him away in a straightjacket, but that she had pretty much forgotten about him until this friend of hers called. Anyway, they're going to go out to his place – it's a small ranch of some sort – and see if they can find his 'treasure,' as she called it."

"Do they think that Parker is there?"

"I don't know what they think. But I asked if I could go with them and she said maybe."

"Maybe? What's that supposed to mean?"

"Maybe means that either I can or I can't."

"Well, when will you know, Paula? God, getting anything out of you is like trying to pour cold molasses out of a cold bottle. Why did she say maybe?"

"She wants to ask Betty Jane. That's the friend."

"When will you know? My god, I should be there. I could bolster my supply. Richard is coming to get me."

"Richard is not coming to get you, Karole. He's looking for Parker. Why, I do not know, but he hoped you would help him find Parker."

"I do hope you're wrong about that, Paula. Anyway, when do you find out?"

"She's going to call me. Probably tomorrow."

"Don't you think I should come down there?"

"Definitely not. Stay where you are."

"Can you get me a few PCBs?"

"What in the world is that?"

"Pampas Cat Balls, of course."

"I'll see what I can do. That's about the last thing on the priority list, if you ask me."

℘

When Polly punched the button for line one, expecting to talk to her former boyfriend, she intoned in a seductive lilt, "Polly speaking."

"Sweetheart, it's Boof," she heard.

Polly truly had become taken with Buford's charm, but she had never for a moment thought of him in a romantic context. He was just a sweet man. Since his disappearance, everybody in the asylum was still on high alert, and Polly did not want it to be known by anyone that she was talking to Boof. "My lord, where are you?" she whispered. "People around here are searching everywhere."

"Have you got your car there, honey?"

"Well, of course. Why would you ask that?"

"I need some help." Buford gave Polly directions to his ranch and told her to get there as fast as she possibly could. "Don't tell anyone why you're leaving," he admonished. "Just leave quietly as soon as you can. I'm in a crisis and I need some fixin'. Now don't tell nobody."

"Well, okay, I guess. I'll have to take you back with me."

"Don't worry honey, we'll deal with that when the time comes. Just steal away and get here as soon as you can."

"Okay, Boof."

Parker's heart sang. He went to the pantry and got down the jar with the *good* marker on it and chopped up one of the testicles and sauteed it in a little butter. He had plenty of pizza left and put the concoction on one slice and covered it up with Parmesan cheese. When he heard a knock on the door, he popped the slice into the microwave oven and waltzed to the door to greet his next beneficiary.

"What's the matter, Boof? What is going on? Why are you here? Lordy, Boof, if anyone knew I was here – if anyone knew *you* were here – we'd both be in trouble."

"Now don't worry about any of that, honey. Here try some of this pizza. Just wait here in the living room, and I'll get us some soda pop while you're eating the pizza."

By the time Buford Parker got back to the living room with the sodas, Polly Kjelson had removed her uniform and was tossing her underwear aside. "Oh, Boof... Boof. I don't know what's come over me." Polly's body was compact and firm and Buford stiffened from anticipation. Quickly as he could, he tore off his shirt while Polly worked on his pants. She was cat-like as she deftly but speedily maneuvered herself into position making mewing noises as she did so. The session lasted all of five minutes, at which time Polly put on some of her clothing and headed out to a destination unknown. As she slammed the door behind her, Parker was on the living room couch, quiet as a still life. Speeding toward Austin in her Toyota Corolla, Polly took the University of Texas exit.

ౠ

The following day a brief article on page three of the American-Statesman appeared under the headline Frat Boys Get Treat:

"From an unidentified source comes word that in a dream-come-true scenario yesterday, a woman showed up at the Beta Alpha fraternity looking for a good time. 'She was a doll,' said the source. 'She walked in the front door and just said she was looking for love. She was polite and dignified about it but wore a couple (of) guys out. Then she disappeared. Nobody knows who she was, but when she first got there, she told us that Boof had fallen asleep. 'He just freaking fell asleep,' she said. The incident was not reported to the police, and has not been confirmed.

Betty Jane saw the article shortly before she left her home for the Hookem House to meet Tina. She knew exactly what it meant.

CHAPTER EIGHTEEN

The non-stop flight from São Paulo to Dallas/Ft. Worth took ten and a half hours. Ricardo Wilson arrived at six-thirty AM Saturday morning having slept soundly for the entire trip with the help of Zolpidem. He passed through immigration and customs twenty minutes before the airport immigration office received a red alert to carefully screen all the incoming passengers named Wilson, as well as those that fit Wilson's description. With his passport and Brazil drivers license, Rico was able to rent a car with minimal questioning. Now, driving southward toward Austin in a metallic blue Honda Civic, he knew that to have arrived in the United States without being identified, he had overcome another monumental hurdle, but he did not know what a close call he had had passing through immigration at the airport. His return to São Paulo was to be from Monterrey, Mexico. If all went according to plan, his buddy, Anatolio Hernandez, would fly him there from Galveston one week hence. Only three days ago, Hernandez had picked up the phone and was utterly astonished to hear Rico's voice. Wilson, not wanting to talk, promised a full explanation if Anatolio would accommodate his need for a stealthy exit. Hernandez, who had once made a solo sailing trip around the world in a thirty-five foot sloop and now got his kicks from flying private forays of questionable legality in his twin engine Cessna, agreed, fully aware that whatever Rico's story was, it would not be boring. Meanwhile, Rico needed to find his old buddy Willy Lopez. Did Willy still live in Austin? Rico was about to find out.

About the same time Rico was arriving in Austin, Michael Chan from the FBI field office in Houston was meeting Coast Guard CDR Billy Joe Bunch at the Austin Airport. All they knew was that Wilson had a US passport. Bunch and Knowland had met several times in DC, and after eliminating several possible destinations had decided to focus on Austin, Texas, which they knew was where Parker lived. They reasoned that the only reason Wilson would risk a trip to the USA would be to contact Parker. It was a long shot, but although they did not yet know it, they had hit the nail squarely on the head.

"Seems like a wild goose chase," Chan said as they walked to the baggage claim area.

"It's worth a shot," Bunch replied. "I can sort of feel him. Like he's somewhere nearby. I have a sixth sense about things like this. I'll tell you something. If I'd gone on the trip we made down to Argentina to find Wilson, we would have found him. They sent a bunch of fly-boys down there with Parker, who knew where Wilson's camp was, but none of em really gave a shit whether they found Wilson or not. It was just an assignment. One of the guys, a jay gee by the name of Williams was scared shitless the whole time they were in camp. It was a god damn Chinese fire drill."

"What is the nature of a Chinese fire drill that separates it from any other?" Chan inquired.

"Come on, Chan, you must know what that is. It's a prank where you stop the car suddenly and everyone gets out and runs around the car a couple times and then jumps back into a different seat. You must have heard of that."

"I *have* heard of it," Chan replied. "I guess I did not know exactly what it meant. We do not use that term in my culture."

"Well, they were in disarray down there. That's all I'm sayin'. They didn't know up from down – shit from shinola – if you know what I mean."

"Maybe chop suey from a fortune cookie?"

"Good one, Chan. Right out of your own culture. Hey you got more on the ball than I thought. Anyway, what I'm telling you is that it was just a bunch of fly-boys on a joyride. That's how I see it, anyways. They didn't care whether they got Wilson or not. The way it turned out was the guide – this guy Buford Parker – did I mention him? – was the one they brought back. Parker! The guide. He got tangled up with some cats or something and it practically killed him from what I hear."

"We are looking for Ricardo Wilson, though, right?"

"Hell yes. Didn't they brief you? Didn't you talk to Bart Knowland? Now there's a guy. You must know that he passed on being Director. A'course you know that. It's your agency, after all. But why wouldn't he want to be Director. FBI Director is one of the top bigshots in federal service. Anyways, I trust that he briefed you on our mission."

"Yes, Mr. Knowland just said to accompany you. He told me you would fill me in."

"Okay. We're here to find Wilson. You got that, right? At least he told you that. Do you carry a piece?"

"Yes. I do."

"Well, I don't. Man, if it comes to gun play, you're the man. I trust you know how to use it."

"From what I know, there will not be any reason to use it."

"Wilson is a big guy, but I'm fast. If he makes a run for it, I can probably run him down. I played some football in college, so I can hold my own, you can count on that, Chan. Ever hear of the Lumberjacks?"

"No."

"Well that's who I played for – the Lumberjacks. Humboldt State. God, what a place. Nothin' like Macon. That's where I'm from. Macon. Macon, Georgia. By the way, did you ever watch any of them old Charlie Chan movies? You're name's Chan, after all."

"No."

"You don't usually think of a Chinaman solving crimes and taking on gang bangers and all that, but Chan was on it. The guy figured out shit. I mean he knew how to solve em. You know what he'd do? He'd figure out the next move, and then he'd be there. Know what I mean?"

"Yes."

"Maybe you're related to him. I suppose there's a lot of Chans around, but you never know, right?"

"Maybe."

"How about Jackie Chan? Are you related to him? Now there's a tough Chinaman. You could be related to him, too. Maybe both Charlie and Jackie. No wonder you're an FBI agent. You come from a tough line. By the way, how'd you get that scar on your face? That's a dilly. You must have been in a knife fight or some damn thing. That's a beaut. How'd the other guy look when you finished with him. I bet you cut him up pretty bad. Well, I'm hopin' that Wilson won't give us much resistance, but if he does, we're ready, wouldn't you say? With my football background and your knife fighting capability, plus you got a piece. We're in good shape. What do you got? A forty-five?"

"Yes."

"Man, this is high adventure. Two tough guys assigned to find and capture a fugitive. The guy thefted a US Coast Guard aircraft. A C-130. How many guys are around who've done that? How many? Take a guess.

"Zero."

"Man I think you hit it exactly. That's if you don't count Wilson, himself. Counting Wilson, it would be one."

Chan did not reply, as the two of them walked out to the Hertz parking lot and found the Ford Focus they had rented.

"Well, what next?" Bunch inquired.

CHAPTER NINETEEN

Betty Jane cut out the newspaper article and dusted off her car before heading for the Hookem House. She got there a couple minutes early and saw that Tina's green Nissan 370Z was already parked. She ordered a small pitcher of margaritas and spotted Tina near the back of the huge building. Tina was sitting with a tall, stately brunette. "This is Paula," Tina announced. Betty Jane greeted her and made it clear from her facial expression that she needed to know what Paula was doing there. Tina filled Betty Jane in on background, to which Paula added some details.

Paula did not mentioned that she had once been Paul, but she did say that it had been she who knocked Parker out so that they could proceed with the rest of the plan. She gave a full account of what they had done, and a bit sheepishly allowed that the entire idea had been hers.

For the first time since Parker was admitted to the hospital two years previously, Tina understood what had happened to him. Tina's face lit up. "He was sexually molested by Pampas Cats," she laughed. "That explains a lot. For example the diagnosis is not found in Merck manual."

Meanwhile, Betty Jane was anxious to add her discovery to the soup pot. "Did you see the article in the paper this morning? she asked.

"Nope, what's up?" Tina asked.

Betty Jane showed Tina the article. "I'm pretty sure I've figured out what happened. This woman somehow knew

Parker, and he gave her one of his special pizzas adorned with Pampas Cat balls. That's what happens."

"What do you mean, 'that's what happens,' Betty Jane? I thought you'd never tried one." Tina shifted in her chair and drained her margarita. "Sorry, I'm just trying to digest all this. I mean maybe you need to fill in a few more blanks."

"There's this girl Trisha who was a friend of Buford's. She was one of the ones who would take care of my cat, Frenzy, when I couldn't. We were not buds, by any stretch, but we were acquaintances and got along okay. Trisha is a golf pro over at the Great Hills Country Club, and she was the first to ever try one of Buford's prize balls. She told me that Buford got a pair from some Chinese apothecary shop run by a sidewalk pharmacist named Wu Li. Trisha was Buford's lucky testee and she had a nice little romp with Buford, but he passed out pretty early on, she told me, and she hadn't got enough. You should hear her talk about how she felt. It's unreal. She gets all animated and just goes on and on. Anyway, she told me that after Buford passed out, she went back to the Country Club and picked up some guy at the 19th hole and gave him the ride of his life. After that, she had to fend this guy off. She told him to bide his time and maybe it would happen again. Of course it never did because Buford got a bad case of cat scratch. So anyhow, that's how come I'm so anxious to go out to Buford's place and snag some. Trisha made the whole experience sound pretty awesome."

෮

Tina was so intrigued that they left the margo pitcher half full and headed out to Buford's ranch in Betty Jane's Buick LeSabre. Upon arriving at the ranch, Betty Jane noticed instantly that the landscape was mostly dead or overgrown.

"Buford usually kept the place pretty well groomed," she said. "Maybe he's not around. I know he used to hang out at the Longhorns' stadium most days, but check it out – it looks like the place has been abandoned."

"What if he's in there? What do we say?" Paula inquired.

"I'm just going to read him out for making me so sick. I'm going to tell him I was so sick that I lost a year of work and that he should pay me back for the lost time."

"Okay, but we're really after some of Parker's stash, right?"

"Damn straight, Tina."

Even though Betty Jane had her story planned, she still thought that a measure of stealth was appropriate. They parked behind a feed shed that had served as a multipurpose storage area for Frenzy's various needs. Betty Jane felt her chest evacuate as she remembered finding her exquisite cat dead. Tina noticed a slight convulsion and asked what happened.

"I just remembered finding Frenzy," she said simply. "Let's take it kind of slow from here."

The three crept around to the front of the house, stooping over as they passed windows at the side. "When he's here, if not outside he's usually in his library," Betty Jane advised.

The front room of the ranch house had a large panoramic window. From the inside there was a view that reached for miles outward toward the Colorado River. Betty Jane peeked in through the edge of the window where there was a gap between the drapes and the window frame.

"He's in there," Betty Jane whispered. "Check it out."

Tina peaked in through the opening and saw Parker for the first time since she had been his nurse. "Looks dead," she said.

Parker was on the living room floor near a leather couch. He was naked, and his clothes were scattered nearby. A couple of pieces of clothing looked as if they were part of a woman's nursing uniform.

"He looks dead, but he's not. He's still passed out from his romp with whoever it was that visited the fraternity boys. Follow me, the back door will be open."

Tina and Paula followed Betty Jane around to the back door and they went in quietly. Betty Jane led them through the dining room to the kitchen. From there Buford's body was in full view and Tina noted that the oozing scratches had healed but had left peculiar scars on his torso. Betty Jane could not bring herself to look at the motionless body. But Paula found some fascination with it and gawked for over a minute at the man she had once KO'd.

"Here's the pantry," Betty Jane whispered. "Look at this," she blurted. There on the top shelf were the quart mason jars of Pampas Cat testicles. On one of the jars was a sticky label with the word *good* written on it with a black marking pen. She grabbed that jar and returned to the kitchen. "I don't think we should take the whole thing. Knowing Buford, he'd be very likely figure out that I was the thief. At least he'd think of it. Do you want some, Paula?"

"No, thanks."

They found some ziplock bags in a drawer, put a dozen PCBs into it, and closed it up. "Tina," Betty Jane said, "You are going to have the time of your life tonight, and it's all going to be enabled by cat balls. You probably don't think you heard me right, but you did. Cat balls."

"Sounds familiar, my friend. Let's get out of here."

"Wait, there's one more thing I have to do."

Betty Jane re-entered the pantry and after a couple of minutes emerged with a smile akin to Lucy's as she, for perhaps the hundredth time, snatched the football away from Charlie Brown.

CHAPTER TWENTY

It was not just that Polly Kjelson knew that she would be lauded as a hero if she were to bring Buford Parker back to Austin State Hospital. She believed with all her heart and soul that that is where he belonged. Her intention when she responded to his call for help was to convince him then and there to return to the asylum with her. She still did not understand, nor could she completely remember, what had overcome her when she stepped into his living room, but whatever it was, it was all behind her. *That was without any question, the most exciting twelve hours of my life. But no matter. I've got a job to do, and I will do it. I've got to go back there and get Boof to come back with me – whatever it might take.*

It was with that resolve that Polly got into her car Sunday morning and started back to Parker's ranch house. It was her good fortune that his original directions were still on the passenger seat. She retraced the route that had taken her to the most bizarre sexual experience she had ever had, almost wondering if it would happen again. Upon her arrival, she parked her car in the loop of the long drive leading to the ranch house, got out, and rang the bell. After several rings and knocks, she left, thinking that Parker was not home.

❧

If he hadn't figured it out already, when CDR Billy Joe Bunch had said, "What next?" Agent Michael Chan became certain that strategic decisions were his to make. "Stop at that gas station," he told Bunch, who was driving.

"It's topped up, Dude. Check out the gauge. It's on the north side of F. That means full. Full up. We can't dally. We've got work to do. I don't think of this as an assignment, I think of it as a mission."

"Pull in."

"Bunch did as he was told and Chan jumped out of the car and bought a map of Austin. When he got back to the car, Bunch was still talking about his obsession to catch Wilson.

"Let's go," Chan directed.

"Where to, Charlie?"

"I got Parker's address and directions to his place. It's that way," indicating eastward.

"Good thinking Charlie. Brilliant. You're going to be an asset. Was that your idea? You're smarter than I thought, pal. Why didn't you just check your phone. There's a voice in there that tells how to get where you want to go. Ever think of that? We're going to get along fine. Man. A map. What a concept."

Billy Joe Bunch continued to rib Chan and jabber all the way out to Parker's place. As they passed the long drive leading into Parker's address they saw three women hastily exiting the side door of the ranch house. Bunch, who was driving the Focus, drove on for five hundred feet and hung a u. As the LeSabre pulled out, Bunch followed behind. "We got 'em now," he said. All we have to do is keep 'em in view, and when they stop, we grab 'em."

"Who do we have? It looked to me like they were all women."

&

"I think we should go back to the Hookem and discuss our caper over a margo or two," Betty Jane suggested.

"I'm in," Tina said.

"Me, too." Paula added. At that moment Paula remembered that she was supposed to call Karole in Ames to bring her up to date. To mention it to the women she was now with would require a lot of background explanation, and besides, she was loving the moment, so she decided to wait.

Betty Jane got a large pitcher of margaritas and they found the same table they had left a couple of hours ago. Shortly after they had sat down Billy Joe Bunch and Michael Chan entered the arena-like bar. The House hushed, and every eye in the House followed the two dark suits to the table the three women had chosen.

"Okay, Girls," Bunch announced with authority, "the jig's up. What are you three up to anyway?"

Tina, visibly shaken, said, "We're having a drink. What do you mean?"

Paula saw the distress in Tina's face. She stood up and said, "It's none of your fucking business, and if you don't beat a hasty retreat you're going to taste some of the sawdust you're standing on."

"Ha ha, that's a good one," Bunch said, just before Paula's bolo punch caught him square on the bottom of his jaw. He did not taste the sawdust because he was out cold. This time a momentary silence in the vacuous bar was followed by a cacophony of murmurs and scattered expletives.

Chan, who liked what he saw, did his best to keep a poker face. "Please forgive us," he said, producing a badge and ID. "That's Commander Bunch, and I'm Special Agent Chan. We're in pursuit of a former Coast Guard officer named Wilson. We don't know if Wilson is here in Austin, but we believe he had business dealings with Buford Parker. We were out there, saw you and followed you here. I think Mr. Bunch was a little over zealous, perhaps, in his haste to talk to you."

Paula said, "Nicely understated, Mr. Chan. Should I douse him with water?"

"I am thinking the interview might go smoother if I talk to you alone," Chan replied. "What was your reason for being out at Parker's house?"

"Mr. Parker was in Brackenridge Hospital a couple of years ago, and I was his nurse. I visit him occasionally to see how he's doing. Betty Jane and Paula are friends. Actually, Betty Jane used to know Mr. Parker. Paula just recently became acquainted with us, so we took her along."

"And how was he? I'm talking about Mr. Parker."

"He's doing nicely," Tina told him.

"So you saw him?" Chan asked.

"Yes, we did."

Chan turned to Paula. "Do you make it a habit to get into fights?"

"No."

"You seem to have a well developed uppercut."

"Your friend is very offensive. I am not a fighter, and I would say that adrenaline took over. I got lucky. Or I *guess* I got lucky – unless I'm in trouble."

"No. I will confirm in my report that Mr. Bunch was offensive."

"Why am I on the floor?" Bunch asked after a minute or two.

"You must have fainted," Tina said. "I'm a nurse. Let me get you some smelling salts." She took his arm to offer help off the floor and Bunch jerked it away.

Bunch rubbed his jaw, which was throbbing. "Did I hit my chin on the way down?"

"Yes," Chan told him.

"That woman threatened me. She must have struck me."

"No, you fainted right after she threatened you. She must have scared you," Tina said. "I repeat. I'm nurse. Let me take you to the hospital."

Bunch looked at Tina in disbelief. He looked at Chan and the other two women, and suddenly realized that everyone in the bar was looking at him, most with enormous grins on their faces. "I did not faint. I don't faint," he said. Bunch then sat down and put his head on the table in front of him.

Chan asked Bunch if he was okay, and when he got no response, continued his line of questioning. All three women were able to frame the trip in a scenario that had nothing to do with Wilson. At one point Chan asked if any of the women knew Wilson. Tina and Betty Jane said they didn't and Paula said nothing.

"I have known Mr. Parker for two years, and in all that time he has never mentioned Wilson to me," Tina told him.

After some fifteen or twenty minutes, Bunch came out of his stupor and entered the discussion. "That does not mean squat. We know that they know each other. We know that Parker went fishing in Argentina with Wilson and that he lead a search party for him down there. Who do you think you're fooling? I think you three are hiding something." And on and on. The words poured forth like hot lava spewing from a volcano. Chan put his hand on Bunch's shoulder, smiled at the three women, and led Bunch back to the Focus. "Maybe we should have a discussion about our strategy, Billy Joe," he said as they got to the car.

"I can't think of a reason in the world that we should be leaving right now, Charlie. Them was some cuties in there. Specially the tall one – the one that threatened me just before I fainted. I don't get it, Charlie. I haven't ever fainted before. Oh well, I think I'm fine now, except for a monster headache. But you can count on me to be ready for whatever develops – or whatever we make develop, wink wink. I do think we ought to go back and maybe offer to take em out to dinner. Jesus H. Christ, we don't want to just leave 'em there. They are obviously looking for company. Chan. Why aren't you talking?"

❧

Although Paula had told her new friends about her role in capturing Buford Parker, they could scarcely believe her quick KO of Commander Bunch. As soon as the interrogation was finished and the men were gone, Betty Jane held Paula's arm in the air and softly enunciated, "Da winnah." The patrons of the Hookem House, mostly students, erupted in applause that lasted for over a minute.

CHAPTER TWENTY-ONE

When Karole's phone rang, she assumed it would be Paula, but it wasn't.

"Hello, Karole, it's Rico Wilson."

"Oh, my god. Richard, are you all right? Oh my gosh, let me sit down. You sound like you're right next door."

"I'm in Texas. Were you able to find out anything about Parker?"

"Texas? Oh my god. Richard, you're in Texas? God I've got to sit down. Where in Texas? My god you're in Texas?"

"Austin. Did you find out anything about Parker?"

"Austin? Oh my god, you're in Austin? That's where Paula is."

"Paula?"

"Yeah, remember Paula? She was supposed to phone me, but she hasn't."

"What's she doing here?"

"She's supposed to be finding Parker."

"Give me her number."

"God, Richard, I should be there with you. I'll get a plane ticket right now. Just stay where you are."

"Don't do that. Just give me Paula's number."

"But you *would* rather deal with me. Paula's great, but... you know."

"I don't know what you mean, Karole. I need to find Parker. I think he's in Austin. I don't really need to talk to you *or* Paula, but if she has been trying to get information I'd like to know what she's found out."

"But you *do* want to *see* me while you're here, Richard."

"Karole, I think you're a peach, but I don't need to see you. In fact, I don't want to. Just give me Paula's number."

"Okay, okay." Karole read the number from her phone. "I'm here if you need me, darling," she said in a pathetic last grope.

"You're sweet, Karole. If I ever make it back to Santos, I'll drop you a card."

"But you don't have my address. Let me..."

"I have it. Take care, my sweet friend."

Karole flopped onto her bed and sobbed off and on for two hours.

℁

During the two years since she had helped with the capture of Buford Parker, Karole had dated only one person. Josh White was an environmental studies graduate student, eight years Karole's junior. While he was an undergraduate, he had won a silver medal in the Olympic downhill and a bronze in the giant slalom. He had also made the USA summer Olympic team as a swimmer and got a bronze in the freestyle relay. Although Karole had pledged her heart to Richard, she found Josh intriguing because of his clever ideas about global health. Josh White had sent perhaps a hundred letters to the President of the United States with copies to many department heads, urging a tax incentive not to have children. In lieu of deductions for dependents, he suggested penalties, as well as tax reductions for not having children, and to the poor – those who had no tax burden to deduct from – annual government payoffs for not having children. He knew that it was an Aryan-like philosophy despised by many, but so what. Everybody should believe in something, he thought. He found little humor in the tee shirt that said, "Everyone should believe in something – I believe I'll have a beer." In fact he found little humor in anything, and that was his shortcoming in Karole's eyes.

While he was a student at Iowa State, Josh had admired Karole, and finally had asked her out after his Olympic success and after he was admitted to the PhD program. Try as he might, he could not get her to make love to him. At this moment Josh did not know the good fortune that awaited him, but he was about to enjoy the most heart rending, amazing, awe inspiring, and memorable afternoon of his life.

Karole's sobbing had stopped with a suddenness that surprised her. *What in God's name have I been doing – fooling myself for the last two years,* she thought. *Richard is a happily married man and he never once gave me any reason to think he was going to forget that for a minute. In fact he told me that over and over. What a fool.* Karole's wishful belief that she was going to ride into the sunset – and give Richard a ride into the sunset – had always subdued her interest in Josh, a guy who had achieved successes that few ever even dream of. Now her own fondest dream had ended just as certainly as if she had crashed in her own attempt at a downhill run. Josh was a good guy. His heart was in the right place even if he might be a little misguided about how to accomplish his goal. *I need to get to know that guy better,* she thought. *He's not an outlaw like my gleaming bronze Adonis. He doesn't steal airplanes, but who does, for goodness sake. Richard is gone. I've got to move on. Maybe I can even get Josh pointed in the right direction. Meanwhile, we're going to have a little fun together.* Karole found the vial that had preserved her little treasure in vodka for two years and punched in Josh White's number.

CHAPTER TWENTY-TWO

During his childhood in Mexico City, Ricardo Wilson's closest friend was Guillermo "Willy" Lopez. Although both of Lopez's parents were Mexican, Willy went to the English speaking school in the capital city and was in the same grade as Richard. They became fast friends almost instantly and used to dream up get-rich-quick schemes together. Richard left Mexico at the age of ten when his family moved to San Diego, but the two boys kept in touch, and on a couple of occasions Willy showed up unannounced at Richard's house. The first time was when Richard was a senior in high school. Willy had inherited ten thousand dollars from his grandfather, and after learning to fly had purchased a used Cessna 210 single engine airplane. The plane was designed to carry six passengers, but Willy took all the seats out and built cages along the sides of the fuselage into which he could fit a hundred baby parrots. He bought the parrots for about twenty-five cents each, US, and flew them to different places in the United States where he got from fifty to seventy-five dollars apiece for them. He also had set up arrangements with consulates and funeral homes to transport the bodies of tourists back to where they were from, and thereby seldom had to undergo a thorough inspection by US Customs. His first four flights were without incident, but on the fifth US Customs discovered the parrots and fined him five thousand dollars. Nevertheless, Willy broke even on the trip.

When Richard started flying TUNAPAT missions, which often took him to Acapulco, Willy showed up with an elaborate plan to smuggle thousands of cartons of Mexican made US brand cigarettes back to San Diego. Willy reasoned that a Coast Guard aircraft would undergo a minimal customs inspection.

At the time Richard was an exemplary officer in the USCG and was not in the least tempted by Willy's scheme. Shortly thereafter Willy had called Richard to tell him that he managed to get most of the cigarettes into the US concealed in a truck shipment of embroidered clothing. A year after that, he called Richard again to say he was living in Austin, Texas where he was booking bets on sports events and practically anything else that his clients were interested in betting on. It was only two months later that that Richard flew southward in a brash exit from San Diego, California and the United States of America.

Even though Richard had told Ingrid that he had a friend in Austin, he doubted that Willy still lived there. When he checked the web he found a few possible hits in Austin, and on the third try he connected with his old buddy.

When Willy Lopez moved to Austin, he bought an empty lot on the outskirts of town and excavated a basement. He then hired a contractor to build a flat roof over the excavation. He covered that with soil and landscaped it. Atop the landscaping he erected a statue of Jeff Kent, a major league ballplayer from Austin. The Kent statue was actually a sophisticated antenna for the state-of-the-art communications systems in the basement which were capable of airing real time action on up to a hundred sporting events.

Willy was swarthy, shorter than average and a bit on the chubby side. His disposition was happy-go-lucky and carefree. Seldom did he do or hear anything that he did not find funny. Although radically different in appearance and attitude, Richard and Willy always called each other *cuate*. When Richard punched in the third Willy Lopez in his list and said, *"Hola Cuate,"* Willy laughed for a full minute before he said a word.

"So, my friend, you are alive and in this country and you need a place to hide out."

"Thrice correct."

Willy laughed for another five or six seconds. "Thrice correct? The fuck is thrice correct?"

"That all three things you guessed are true. Come on, Willy."

"Hey, *mi estimado amigo,* what in the hell are you up to now? You were all over the news a few years back. I was proud of you, *Cuate.* Stealing a plane from the government? Man, that was cool. You got balls, man. Even I wouldn't have thought up that one. What else have you done? Hey, I could really use a plane like that. What'd you do with it?"

"Listen Willy, I'll bring you up to date, but you're right, I need a place to lay low for a few days. Can you help me out?"

"Shit yes, *Cuate,* any time. Come on over man. I live in a hideout anyhow. You're going to like it here. I'll come and get you. Just stay put."

"I gotta tell you where I am, Willy."

"No you don't, man, I got you pinpointed on my radar. I got everything down here."

"Jesus, Willy, I hope the government's equipment isn't as good as yours."

"It's not, *Cuate,* I got the best stuff."

Fifteen minutes later Richard was in Willy's cave. He compressed the essence of his last five years into the time it took to get to Willy's "home."

&

The entrance to Willy's cave was located in the kitchen of a Burger King franchise that he owned. A block long tunnel led to the "combat center," as he called it. Rico took it all in in silent awe, as Willy showed him the equipment that made up the heart and circulatory system of his endeavors.

"You're only the eighth person who has ever been down here. Two of those were guys I hired to help set this stuff up."

"How often do you leave?"

"Not often, my friend. I love it down here."

"How do you get paid?"

"Come on, man. Everything's automatic. Direct deposits, mostly to El Banco de Commercio in Monterrey. Automatic currency conversion, the whole marianne. I've got a couple banks here that I can transfer in and out of. I love what I do. You should join me. There's plenty of work for two of us in this set up."

"I'd go nuts living down here in your cave, Willy. Besides I've got a mission to accomplish, and then I'm headed back to Santos. I love it there."

"Okay. You told me what you did. What's your so-called mission?"

"I'm owed a million bucks by the guy who I collected the cat balls for. I intend to squeeze it out of him."

"I can help you there, *Cuate.*"

"I have to think I'm on every enforcement list in the USA. That being the case, I would not be a good guy to partner up with right now. You've got a secure spot here, and for some reason I can't begin to fathom, you don't mind being holed up in it. I'd go bonkers if I had to spend more than a day or two down here."

"Well, shit, *Cuate,* where do I fit in?"

"Right where you are. If I can stay here a couple days and try to coordinate some stuff, I'll take care of my business and take off. I've got a route to Santos set up. I'm happy there, man. I've got a wife you couldn't take your eyes off of. You should visit us sometime."

"I'm a mole. Seldom see the daylight. When I picked you up it was probably my first trip out in over a month. The shades I wear are not so I'll be incognito. They're so I'm not blinded by the sun."

"God, you must get lonely down here all by yourself."

"Hey, gimme a break, I don't get lonely because my girlfriend comes down almost every night. She's a sports fan. We watch games together. Drink expensive wine. She helps me with posting odds. We get a lot of action because our line doesn't always match the Vegas line. I have a lot of line shoppers. They hedge their bets to improve their chances. I don't care. I get more business that way. Our lines are usually closer than the pros'. That's all we do. If I get a bet so big that losing it would hurt me, I just cover it with my own bet somewhere else. Is it rocket science? God damn right it is. And it ain't for the faint of heart. But me and Lil love it. Lil's short for the 'little lady.'"

"Is she coming tonight? Will I be in the way?"

"I don't know. But you won't be in the way. She'll think you're cool. I mean how many guys do what you did?"

"I gotta make a call, *Cuate*. Can I do it from here?"

"Get on it, man. You can do anything you want from here. And when action time comes, count me in. I have never decided against something because there was a risk involved. It looks to me like you may have turned over that same leaf."

CHAPTER TWENTY-THREE

The trio at the Hookem House was still sipping their refilled margaritas when Paula's phone rang.

"Paula, it's Richard Wilson."

"Not likely. Who is it?"

"Richard, your fishing guide in Argentina."

"Come on. Who is it really. I don't like pranks."

Betty Jane intervened. "Who is it, Paula?"

"Whoever it is thinks he's Richard."

"Maybe it is," Betty Jane and Tina said together.

"It *is* Richard," Richard repeated.

"How did you know I'd be here?"

"I don't know where you are. I got your number from Karole."

"I can't believe it. You talked to her? She's bonkers over you, Richard."

"I know. It's not my doing. I'm just trying to find Parker."

"We just saw him. I mean we just came from there. I'm at the Hookem House with Betty Jane and Tina. You don't know them, but they both have had occasion to deal with Parker. Neither is real fond of him at the moment, I'd say."

"You saw Parker? How did you know where he was?"

"Yeah, we saw him. He's passed out on the floor in his living room. Betty Jane knows where his ranch is. She's the one who did all the chemistry on the Pampas Cat attraction serum, or whatever it was. Betty Jane thinks Parker gave some gal a dose of his love potion and whoever it was wore him out."

"Does she have any reason to think that?"

"Well, yeah. It's a long story."

"Tell it."

Paula gave Richard a full account of the newspaper article, their afternoon foray to the ranch, and the visit from Bunch and Chan. In the detailed narrative, she included her dispatch of the Coast Guard Commander, noting that it was in the same manner she had dealt with Parker two years previously. She was so detail rich in telling it that Richard had to keep telling her to get on with it.

"First I want to say bravo for the job on Bunch. Fine piece of work. But what's your interest, and what's their interest? Why did you go out to Parker's place? What are you three trying to accomplish?"

"Well, first, Betty Jane wanted to get a few nuggets – you know, for her own use. That was number one on our agenda. Since Betty Jane made the bait stuff, she knew why Parker wanted it, and she knew what it did. So as soon as your shipment arrived from Argentina, she was going to have a go at it with Parker. Well, as it turned out, she almost died. It turned out that he had a batch that was poisoned. We kind of guessed that you might have had a hand in that."

"I did, but I didn't know they would act like poison. I just thought that they would be benign. When I started to suspect that I was not going to get paid for my efforts, I just sent him a bunch of leftovers from an animal clinic in Buenos Aires where they neutered cats."

"Well, Betty Jane told me that she and Buford each had one and they thought they were going to die. Puked all night, she said."

"Well, it's music to my ears that Parker got sick, but I'm sorry to hear about Betty Jane. As I remember she was the chemist who reproduced the pheromone."

"Right, and she is still livid about it. At first I thought she wanted to kill him, but I think she just wanted to get some of the treasure. As I told you, she – or should I say *we* – did."

"There's little doubt that her getting sick was my doing. Apologize to her for me."

"She's not mad at you. Just Parker."

"She is still owed an apology. Sounds like a pretty grim experience."

"I'll pass it along to her, Richard."

"Any idea how the g-men found you?"

"No. We had just got our margos – that's what Tina and Betty Jane call margaritas – and they were in our face."

Richard considered all he had heard. "Listen, Paula, if I were to make a guess, it would be that those two goons are surveilling you right now. I wonder what in the hell tipped them off that I was here. I only just decided a week ago to come up here. My god, I thought I was under the radar. I'm going to have to lay low for awhile. They're probably staked out somewhere so that the door of your place is in view, Paula. Where are you staying?"

"I'm at a motel. Tina and BJ live here."

"Okay, if you leave, they're going to follow you. They would spot me in an instant. I'm going to lay low for a couple days. At some point they will give up on following you around and we can meet somewhere. I have some business to transact with Parker. Are you all in the same car?"

"No. We all met up here in our own cars. Mine's a rental, but they have their own."

"When you leave, see if you can spot them. They'll have to make a choice about which one of you to follow. If you do see them let me know. Is my number on your phone?"

Paula looked at her phone. "Yep, there it is."

"It's a throw-away. Keep the number. I don't know how long I'll be here – by here I mean in the US – but I'll have this phone the whole time. Keep me posted, okay? I'll never forget the uppercut you laid on Parker. Sorry I missed the one on Bunch. Thanks, Paula. You are one fine friend."

"Ten-four, Sweetheart. I'll be in touch."

&

It was not difficult for the three young women to spot the car that Bunch and Chan were watching the door from. By agreement none of them acknowledged the sighting and they each strolled to the car they had arrived in.

"Which one?" Bunch asked.

"The blonde," Chan answered, starting up the Focus.

"I don't feel so good," Bunch said.

"You look a little peaked."

"What the hell does that mean?"

"Rough around the edges. You took quite a fall in there."

"That girl didn't hit me, did she? I've never fainted before."

"No, Bunch, you got pale and fell against the table – or maybe the back of the chair. Anyway, your head snapped back like you'd been clobbered by an uppercut."

"I gotta rest. When we stop I'm going to get out and get in the back seat," Bunch moaned.

"Sort of like a Chinese fire drill?"

Bunch did not smile. "Sort of."

They followed Betty Jane at a distance. As she watched them in the rear view mirror, she noticed that Bunch exited the car and re-entered while they were stopped at a stoplight. *What the hell was that,* she thought.

Betty Jane saw the Focus stop a block back of her when she pulled into her garage. *What's next,* she wondered.

"I think that one knows more than she told us," Chan said to the beaten looking Bunch. "I'm going to ask her a few more questions. Are you in?"

"Not in," Bunch said. "I think you're wasting your time. In fact I'm going back to the hotel. Call me when you're done and I'll pick you up."

"Okay, if that's what you want. It might only take ten minutes or so."

"I'll wait ten here. If you're not out, I'll assume you hit on something important and go back to the hotel. If that happens, call me when you're finished talking to her."

"Fair enough."

Michael Chan's parents were Han Chinese from the Hakka region of southern China. His father was over six feet tall and Chan was six-two. He was strong and fit, having run and lifted for most of his adult life. The scar on his face had come from an attack from Ignacio "Nacho" Maldonado, a Mexican drug lord who had crossed the border to set up a ring of cocaine outlets in El Paso. Chan had attempted to place Maldonado under arrest and before he knew it he was slashed across the cheek by Maldonado's dagger. Chan was an expert at Silat, a deadly Philippine martial arts form that he had practiced since his early childhood. In a move that would have made Chan's namesake, Jackie, shudder with awe, Chan had quickly unleashed a side kick to Maldonado's neck that killed him instantly.

He knocked on Betty Jane's door and waited only moments before she opened it in feigned surprise. "May I come in?" he asked.

"Sure, I guess," she said. "Can I get you something to drink?"

"Water would be good."

"How about a coke?"

"Sounds good."

Betty Jane poured half a can of coke into each of two glasses. She quickly extracted one Pampas Cat testicle from the baggie she had collected the specimens in, minced it up, and added some chocolate syrup. She put half the syrup into each coke glass with shaved ice and took them out to the room

99

where Chan was waiting. "Try this," she said. It's my new concoction."

If the *cojones* changed the taste of the drink at all, it was so little that it was not discernible, and because the two of them drank it slowly, the sexual excitement did not occur suddenly. Betty Jane knew what was coming, but Michael Chan was taken by surprise. Betty Jane was a beautiful and charming young woman, but Chan was there to get information.

"Are you sure that Mr. Parker, in all the time you knew him, never mentioned Coast Guard Commander Wilson at any time?"

"Yes, sir, Mr. Chan."

"In all the time you knew him, did he ever mention your incredibly fine body? God you're the sexiest thing I've ever seen in my entire life. Jesus, did I actually say that? Well, forgive me, but it is true. You are amazing."

"Mr. Chan, you might want to see this fine body with less clothing hiding it, don't you think?" Betty Jane said as she removed her shirt.

"That was probably your best idea yet. May I call you sweetheart?"

"Yes. Please do." Betty Jane took off her pants and moved to the couch where Chan was sitting.

Chan kissed her softly and took off his shirt. "I'm sorry sweetheart, I don't know what's happening."

"I do," Betty Jane said softly. "It is a result of my hard work in the chem lab. I will explain it all to you tomorrow morning."

No further words were spoken. Betty Jane's research had finally paid off, and with a man far, far sexier than Buford Parker would have been or ever could be. The dose of half a ball each proved to be perfect for a long, enduring, affectionate, but active love making session. Chan's phone rang a couple of times, and he knew that it was Billy Joe Bunch. What Michael Chan was doing was more important than Billy Joe. In the orange dawn of the morning, Chan proposed marriage to Betty Jane.

"No," she said simply, "but we will see each other from time to time."

"Whatever came over us, or overcame us, I hope that it might happen again. I have many cherished moments in my memory, but this tops them all."

CHAPTER TWENTY-FOUR

Monday morning Michael Chan phoned Bunch. "Just wanted to let you know that I'm finished with the interrogation. I'd appreciate it if you'd come by and get me."

"I can't remember how to get there."

Chan gave him directions, and Bunch was there fifteen minutes later. The good-byes between Chan and Betty Jane were affectionate and filled with anticipation of future encounters. When Chan saw the Focus come into view he descended the front stairs with a bounce in his step that had been missing for years.

"You fucked her, you unprofessional lowlife," Billy Joe said.

"Mr. Bunch, I got some information that will guide me in this pursuit. If you make any more comments about what you think I might have done while I was there, you will not be happy that you did so."

"Are you threatening me?" Bunch asked incredulously.

"Yes."

Bunch was obsessed about catching Ricardo Wilson, and this turn of events made him boil inside. Not only had Bart Knowland sent a Chinaman to partner up with him, but this guy clearly had his own agenda. Bunch began to consider how he should proceed, given this loathsome development.

"Where do we go from here, Charlie?" he asked icily.

"Back to the bar we were at. The Hookem."

"Why back there, for chrisakes?"

"Just do it."

"I don't just do stuff because you say to, Charlie. We have to keep surveillance on these women, At the moment they're all we have."

Chan knew that Bunch was right. "Okay. We can watch the house for awhile, at least while we decide what to do. Listen, you stay here and I'll go back in and get some answers that that woman refused to give me the first time around."

"Are you serious? You expect me to believe that?"

"It's all you got, dude."

Bunch was overcome with hatred for this man. "We're supposed to be tracking down a guy who stole one of our aircraft. Chan, do you have any idea what a C-130 is worth?"

"No. Do you?"

"Hell yes, I do. The one he took with wingtip tanks and sophisticated nav gear and rescue equipment'll run ya around fourteen mil. In case you're wondering that's more than you and I would make in ten lifetimes."

"I do know we're on a mission, Little Buddy. I've got to go back in there and clear up a couple of things."

Killing Chan was not an option. To keep in shape, Bunch regularly ran four miles every other day, and he had the slender body that runners often have, but not only did he give away forty pounds to the chisel-bodied Chan, he was not aware that Chan held a tenth degree black belt in Silat. Commander Billy Joe Bunch felt defeat overcoming him.

"Go ahead," he said. "Go do whatever it is you're doing up there. I'll wait."

Although only a commander, Bunch was on a mission that was in the top ten of the US Coast Guard's priority list. As a consequence he had a direct line to Admiral Gene Skilling, Vice Commodore of the Coast Guard. As soon Chan was out of the car, he quick-dialed Skilling.

"This is Commander Bunch, sir."

"Mr. Bunch, how goes the pursuit?"

"It goes bad, sir. Did Mr. Knowland discuss this mission with you? For example, did you have any input into who I would be working with?"

"No names, Mr. Bunch. He mentioned that the FBI had a field office in Houston. As I remember he was pretty enthusiastic about his staff there. He was going to try to get a guy who was proficient in martial arts, although every report we have on Wilson suggests that Wilson is not a fighter."

"Well, so far our only lead has been three women who we are certain are acquainted with Parker. We think Parker is Wilson's target or reason for coming to the United States. But as far as I know, we still don't even know if Wilson is in the country. Have you had any confirmation of that, one way or the other, sir?"

"No. I'll see if Knowland has heard anything. Is there anything I should know if I talk to him?"

"There sure is, sir. This guy spent the night with one of our subjects of interest."

"Any idea what he was doing, Mr. Bunch?"

"Yes, sir. I do have an idea."

"Go ahead, Bunch."

"Sir, this woman is about thirty-five years old and is a real knockout. It appears to me that they might have hooked up. What I mean is that for whatever reason they put pleasure before business."

"That's a pretty audacious accusation, Mr. Bunch"

"When Charlie called me to pick him up, he wanted us to leave together and go back to this bar where we first encountered the subjects of interest."

"Who is Charlie?"

"Uh, sorry, sir, that's what I call Chan. He's a Chinaman."

"What were you doing that he had to call you to pick him up?"

"I had left him at the house where I think he was having sex with the blonde."

"Why weren't you there together, Mr. Bunch?"

"I had fainted and hit my chin. I wasn't feeling so good."

"Fainted?"

"Yes. I fainted. That's what they told me, anyway. I've never fainted before. I still don't know exactly what happened. I was just talking to this tall girl and I passed out. Hit my chin on something, and I was feeling real sick."

"Mr. Bunch, in your view was the tall girl a knockout also?"

"No, sir. I mean she was not a bad looking girl at all. Just not a knockout like the blonde. She had kind of an androgynous look about her."

"Androgynous? What about the other girl?"

"Sir, they were in a bar drinking margaritas, I think. I was just going to interrogate them and I passed out. Fainted. Hit my chin."

"Okay, Mr. Bunch. Thanks for the call. I trust you'll do whatever it takes to keep from fainting."

&

Betty Jane was surprised to see Chan back at her door only moments after he had left. "What's up?" she asked.

"I told my partner that I had to get a few more answers out of you. He's really steamed. I really do need some answers, Betty Jane."

Chan went to the living room with Betty Jane and they sat down on the couch where their marathon love-making session had started. "Michael, I knew what was happening last night, and you didn't."

"Of course I did. I was half the equation."

"To use your terms, there was a part of the equation that you don't understand. I knew what was going to happen. Maybe I should have warned you, I don't know. I don't even know if I should explain it all to you."

"As you know, we are pursuing Richard Wilson. The reason we want him is that he stole a Coast Guard airplane. He is wanted by the Coast Guard and the FBI among others, and I am the FBI agent that is assigned to catch him. You and the other two women who we talked to claim not to know Wilson. Is that correct?

"No."

"You know him?"

"No, but Paula does. I can tell you with certainty that she would never give him up. I expect she would kill herself before she would tell you anything. You saw what she did back at the Hookem. She is an unusual woman. I don't know where she lives, so I can't help you in your pursuit of Wilson."

"I'm not going to pressure you, Betty Jane, but out of respect for your country, you should tell me anything that might help me apprehend Wilson."

"I love my country, but I can continue to do that without helping you. I can also continue to admire you, and cherish the memory of last night without helping you. I must say, we all noticed that you took our side in explaining what happened to Mr. Bunch when Paula hauled off on him."

"That was simply a case of not liking the man. I do, however, take my mission seriously. I just wish I was carrying it out with someone other than Bunch."

"Michael, I'm not sure that this is the time to fill you in on some background. Let me think it over and when we meet again I'll know if it's appropriate or not."

CHAPTER TWENTY-FIVE

Polly was obsessed with bringing Buford Parker back to Austin State Hospital. She actually missed his company, but she also felt a responsibility for his disappearance. Although not a word had been said to her about it, she was certain that there was talk among the staff that she had in some way facilitated his disappearance. She needed to bring Parker back. As she was drifting off to sleep she contrived the idea of taking Doowite out to Parker's ranch so that if Parker resisted, Doowite could help her subdue him. The following day she stopped Doowite in the hallway as he emerged from his morning conference with Moon Muenter.

"Excuse me, Doowite," she said shyly.

"Huh?"

"Um… I said, excuse me. Could I speak to you for a minute."

"Yeah. Yeah, you could speak to me for a minute." Doowite laughed out loud.

"I'm sorry, Doowite, but I think I might know where Mr. Parker is, and I wondered if you'd go there with me to get him and help me bring him back."

"You think you know where Parker is? Well, that's a good one, Miss, uh, what's your name anyway?

"Don't you even know my name? It's Polly."

"Yeah, I knew that, but I don't know your last name."

"Oh, it's Kjelson. It's Swedish. Polly Kjelson."

"Well then, Miss Kjelson, you want me to go get Parker with you?"

"Yes. Uh huh, if you wouldn't mind."

"Okay. I'll do that."

After a quick discussion about what to tell their supervisors, they decided to wait until the lunch hour and make the trip on their break. They got there around 12:20 and there was no sign of life.

"What makes you think Parker is here?" Doowite asked.

"Well, I did some checking around."

"Checking around."

"Yes, I checked around. Mr. Parker is in the phone book."

Polly peeked through the widow and could see that Parker was no longer on the floor where she had last seen him. She knocked on the door and was surprised when it opened.

"Well, gawleee, look who's here. Come in. Come in, heah?"

"Mr. Parker... uh.."

"Come in Doowite. Come in Polly." Parker showed Doowite an extended index and pinkie. "Hookem, baby." he said, in disbelief that Doowite Jackson was in his house. "Come in, Doowite. Sit down right here."

"Sir, we're going to ..."

Parker suddenly realized that he was not getting a social call. "Sit down there just a minute. Wait here." He knew what he had to do and even the realization nauseated him. But it was his own skin that was in grave danger at this moment. He retrieved a Pampas Cat ball from the *good* jar, minced it up with some butter and spread it on a couple pieces of toasted sourdough bread. "Here," he said, "try these. I just got the bread from the farmers market less than an hour ago."

Doowite and Polly were indeed hungry and ate the offering without commenting on the strange flavor. Within two or three minutes they both had their clothes off.

Prior to her afternoon with Parker and four fraternity boys, Polly had only had sex twice, both times with Donny Ray. Donny Ray had a hair trigger, and Polly didn't remember much about the strange afternoon with Parker, et al. This is to say, she was neither a veteran, nor an accomplished practitioner when it came to sex. When she looked at Doowite's cock she realized that this was going to be no ordinary moment in her life, and it wasn't. Before Doowite had finished, Polly had produced three operatic crescendos that vibrated the Baccarat crystal inside Parker's bar room cabinets. Parker watched this extreme show of passion in envy, but knew that he could never measure up even if he downed a couple of cat balls himself. He put his hand inside his trousers. It was like reaching into an old baitbox containing a dried up worm. *Oh my, oh my,* he thought. *What a revolting situation. But at least they won't take me away. They shouldn't anyway. They'll be beholden to me. God, look what I've done for those two people. They probably never looked at each other before and now they're fucking their brains out as if they were long lost lovers. Oh my.*

CHAPTER TWENTY-SIX

Betty Jane timed her call to reach Tina during her lunch break. "Well, they work," she said. "We got the right batch."

"Betty Jane! How do you know? I mean if you know, you must have tried one. Who was the lucky man?

"Michael Chan, our local FBI agent."

"And he went nuts?"

"We both did. Half a nut each. Perfect."

"Chan, my god, BJ, you're playing with the wrong team."

"Listen, I don't know if I am or not. Chan hates Bunch, but he is still pretty intent on capturing our heroic pilot."

"How much did you tell him?"

"Not much. I wanted to talk to you first."

"That's a call you have to make yourself, BJ. There's no way I can tell what your relationship is like. I mean did you feel an affectionate attachment, or was it like having sex with Buford?"

"Well, Chan is a sweet guy, and very sexy. And what a body! I've never seen such a thing. But he wants to capture Richard. I don't even know Richard, but Paula says he's like a big puppy dog. She would shelter and protect that guy with her very life."

"We have to keep our focus, BJ. We want to get even with Parker. We have no reason to care one way or the other about Wilson. But he has never hurt us, and after all he was the original supplier of the magic morsels that you finally, after all your research, got to experience. I'm happy for your. Can't wait to get the details."

"You know what I've been thinking, Tina? Maybe I could use the equipment at the laboratory to duplicate the aphrodisiac itself. You know, whatever it is in the testicles that is the big turn-on. That would cut out a couple of middle men. Maybe we could go into business with Wu Li. That's the guy who originally had the pair of Pampas Cat balls that he sold to Parker. I think Buford paid the guy five thousand dollars for them. I'm not sure I could do it, but I duplicated the essence of Pampas pussy pussy, after all."

"My god, how cool would that be. I've got three or four in a baggie. I'm trying to get up the nerve to try one. I haven't decided who to invite to the party."

"Make sure it's not Bunch."

"Not a chance. By the way, have you talked to Paula?"

"No, but I need to. She may have an update from Richard by now."

ℰ

Paula's phone jingled. "Hey, Betty Jane."

"Hi, Paula. Any more news from our favorite airplane thief?"

"Nope. He told me that he's going to lay low for a few days. I don't know where he's at, but he wants to hide out until he's sure that there's no dragnet out for him."

"Will you be talking to him again?"

"Yeah, no doubt."

"Okay, tell him that I tried one of the balls from the jar that had the *good* sticker on it. Tell him it was, indeed, good. Also, tell him that I put the *good* label onto one of the other jars. So the one with the *good* label could be either good or bad. I doubt he needs to know that, but in case he should have the opportunity to get his hands on some, he'll have the info."

"I knew you did something while we were there. I could tell by the grin on your face when you came out of the pantry. Good one. The only trouble is now we don't know which jar for sure has the good ones in it." *God, I wonder who she shared the treasure with. I can't ask. Too personal.*

"You're right. How stupid of me. My god, we're worse off then when we started. At least we knew which jar had the good ones. I really should have taken the whole jar. If we ever go after any more we'll have to keep in mind that we don't know which are which. So anyway, are you going to tell Richard where Parker's ranch house is?"

"If he asks, I'll tell him."

"Okay, Paula. Keep in touch."

₭

Paula considered her situation. She was in a motel, and all appearances suggested that neither Chan nor Bunch knew it. She also was confident that since Chan had covered for her knockout punch, that she would not likely be pursued. The g-men had followed Betty Jane. *Was it because she was the prettiest,* she wondered. *Well, it didn't matter. That's who they followed. That's all that mattered. My god! Could it be that Betty Jane's testicle experiment was with Chan or Bunch? She wouldn't do that. Or would she? There wasn't much time to corral someone else. If it was one of them, I hope it was Chan. God, that Bunch character is a real dork.*

Paula quick-dialed Richard. When he picked up she said, "I have a couple tidbits for you. Nothing big, but I just thought I should bring you up to date."

"What's up, Paula?"

"Well, one – the two goons followed Betty Jane, so Tina and I are not under surveillance. And two, Betty Jane wanted me to tell you that she tried one of the balls we swiped from Buford, and it worked as it was supposed to."

"Wow. Did she give you any details? Like did she tell you who the lucky guy was?"

"Nope. Just that it worked. The jar we got our little supply from had a sticky label marked *good* She wanted me to tell

112

you that she put peeled it off and put it onto a different jar. So the jar that says good now might be good or it might be the one that poisoned her."

"I'm glad to hear that Betty Jane finally got to try the right kind. Do you two get along?"

"Yeah, she's great. – a real beauty. Even prettier than Karole."

"I talked to Karole, by the way. She was still harboring hopes that I'd want to run off with her."

"Poor Karole. If you'd like I'll check up on her and let you know how she's doing."

"Best not, Paula."

"Are you safe?"

"You'd be amazed if you saw where I'm staying. Yeah, I'm safe."

"Ever thought about going back to the Riachuelo Gato?"

"How could I not."

"If you do, I'd like to go, too. Such a place."

"I'll keep you in mind, Paula.

"One more thing, Richard."

"What's that?"

"I'm sure I could retrace the way to Buford's ranch, so if you should wish to go out there, I can show you the way."

"I'll keep that in mind, too."

CHAPTER TWENTY-SEVEN

Michael Chan was in a conundrum. He was pretty sure that Betty Jane was hiding something. In fact the way the three women at the Hookem House answered his questions led him to believe that all three were not coming across with the whole story. He also was mystified by the sudden wild sexual interlude that he had experienced with Betty Jane. *I could get into that again,* he thought. *In fact maybe I should disqualify myself from this mission and just hang with Betty Jane for awhile. That wouldn't be such a bad life, would it? I wonder if she's always that way. She didn't act like it when I was talking to her at the Hookem House. In fact, in the morning she seemed a little circumspect. I don't know what to think about my new lover. Right now she appears to be obstructing justice. That is what I need to keep in mind.*

Commander Bunch was in the adjoining motel room. As much as Chan despised the man, he knew that they needed to work together to have the best chance of capturing Wilson. Chan punched the quick-dial key for Bunch.

"Bunch."

"This is Chan. Listen, we need to work together in our pursuit. I was wrong to spend the night with Betty Jane and I apologize. Maybe we can put that behind us and work together."

"Maybe. What do you suggest, Charlie?"

"I think we need to go out to Parker's place and talk to him. Maybe he can point us in the right direction."

"Chan, I read the report that the fly-boys wrote up after their fiasco two years ago. One thing that was noted repeatedly is that Parker hated Wilson. The skipper on the flight was CDR Tim Taylor. He was the only one in the party with a brain. Anyway, he wrote in the report that he thought Parker wanted to kill Wilson. No reason was given, or even speculated."

"Well, if he hates Wilson, maybe he'd be a useful ally."

"He was a disaster on the Argentina trip. No respect for authority, had his own agenda, went AWOL and came back so drunk he couldn't walk. My thinking is to leave him to his own devices. We might want to stake out his place or something. I mean the reason we picked Austin to look for Wilson is that Parker is here."

"I have to admit, you're making sense, Bunch. We'd better organize a plan pretty quick. Our bosses are going to want a status report before long, I expect."

"Maybe we should go back and question the blonde some more. This time I could be the guy who does it. I want to see what happens in there."

"That's not a good plan."

"Okay, what is?"

"I think the tall woman who threatened you knows the most. Why would she get upset if she didn't know anything."

"I didn't really faint in there, did I?"

"Yes. You fainted."

"I like the plan, but we don't know where she lives. Come to think of it the only one we know where she lives is the blonde. You fucked that babe, didn't you? What else could've you done there for a whole night?"

"I was trying to get information. I have not forgotten that we are here to apprehend Wilson."

"Jesus, we are not going about this very professionally. I thought the FBI was super organized."

Chan thought for a few seconds, then said, "About the only useful thing we know is where Parker lives. We also know where Betty Jane lives, but she doesn't know Wilson – at least that's what she said. I think we have to go back out to Parker's place and just stake it out. Maybe Wilson will show up. Or maybe he'll go to Wilson."

"Let me have a shot at Betty Jane. If she charmed you, she'll probably charm me. I won't let her. I'll find out what she knows."

"I really did interrogate her, Bunch. She doesn't know anything."

"Take me over there. We'll see if you're right."

"Okay, but it's a waste of time. We should be watching Parker's place."

"Maybe that's next."

Billy Joe Bunch bounded up the stairs with great anticipation. After getting no answer to his knocking and ringing, he returned to the car feeling impotent and defeated.

℘

At the time Bunch was knocking at her door, Betty Jane was at the laboratory working on a non-opioid pain medication that the university was developing. On her lunch break she ran a spectrograph on one of the PCBs, which she had decided to sacrifice for her project. The graph indicated a chemical formula for what Betty Jane discovered through a computer search was a mertestate. However, there was a polymeric difference between the mertestate and the PCB. Betty Jane was a sophisticated research chemist, but the molecule she was looking at was not in any database she could find on line. To her disappointment, it seemed doubtful that she would be able to reproduce this unusual organic compound.

The diversion of her phone ringing was a relief. It was Tina. "Hey, bud, I tried one."

"Really? Really? When?"

"Yesterday."

"Who was the lucky guy?"

"Ronald Talbot."

"Do I know Ronald?"

"Nope."

"Well, who is he?"

"Kind of an interesting story actually."

"Well, are you going to tell it, or did you just call to whet my curiosity?"

"I'll tell it." A long silence ensued. "Just between us. Don't tell a soul."

"Get on with it, Tina."

"Okay, this guy comes into the hospital. He's well tanned, dark hair, blue eyes, he's wearing shorts and a Hawaiian shirt. Really nice looking guy."

" 'What are you here for?' say I".

" 'Erectile dysfunction,' he tells me."

" 'You have ED?' I ask. 'How old are you?' "

" 'Thirty-four,' he says."

" 'Have you seen a therapist?' I ask. 'At your age you should not have ED unless there's a mental aspect to it.' "

" 'Nope, this is my first stop,' he says."

"So I start wondering if these magic marbles might cure this guy's trouble. So I tell him I have a sex therapy office but it's in a different place. 'In fact it's in my home,' I tell him."

"Long story short, we go out to my place. I tell him to wait in the rec room while I get the medicine ready. It so happens that I had some leftover pizza, so I used the tried and true delivery system, and it cured him."

"What? No details?"

"Nope. I used your recipe – half a nut each. Whirled it up with some Parmesan cheese and voila. 'Here's the cure,' I said. Just have a slice of pizza.' So he downs it and, as I say, it worked."

"But, Tina, you're a nurse. You're supposed to cure your patients, not just give them the best ride this side of the mechanical longhorn at the Hookem House."

"He's cured. I just told him to eat some pizza when he wanted to get it up. It'll be the placebo effect."

"Ya think?"

"No doubt about it, bud. The guy's cured."

CHAPTER TWENTY-EIGHT

Bunch and Chan staked out Parker's place for ten hours and saw nothing. There was no sign of anyone coming or going, or even opening a door, so they gave up.

"We have to talk to him," Chan said on the way back to their motel.

"Okay. That's what we'll do tomorrow."

"We could go back and do it now."

"No, we've put in our work for the day. We want to be in good form when we talk to him."

"Good form?"

"Yeah, we might be too tired to do a good job. Tomorrow we'll have a fresh start. We'll be coffeed up and rarin' to go."

"Bunch, there's something I should say about working with you."

"What's that, Charlie?"

"It really sucks. I mean you are so fucking random that I don't see how you ever made commander."

"Well, Charlie, when I look at you, I don't see Mr. Wizard. You're a disgrace to the heroic Chans."

"Okay, it appears that we are not ideally suited to work together, but we have to. So we will. Tomorrow we will talk to Mr. Parker."

The next morning after finishing off a grand slam breakfast at Denny's, the partners headed out to Buford Parker's ranch. Buford had not ventured outside since his successful escape, but he needed to get groceries soon or he wouldn't last. At the same time as Chan turned into the driveway, Parker's garage door was opening.

"That's gotta be him," Bunch said. "He's already seen us, so we can't follow him."

"We came out here to talk to him, so that's what we'll do." Chan pulled the car into the turn-around loop and stopped in front of the garage door. Bunch jumped out of the car and ducked under the garage door, which was now closing.

"Mr. Parker?" Bunch said.

Parker looked at Bunch and did not recognize him as an Austin State Hospital staffer, but still was apprehensive. "Buford Parker," he said. "And who might you be?"

"My name is Commander Billy Joe Bunch, US Coast Guard," Bunch announced proudly.

"The fuck? You are willing to admit that you are affiliated with the Coast Guard? You guys almost killed me. I was within a gnat's eyelash of succumbing because you failed to protect me from our mutual enemy."

"Sir, I don't think you can blame me, or even the Coast Guard for that. I understand that you were not cooperative on the mission." At that point there was a banging on the garage door. "That's my partner from the FBI. We best let him in."

Parker pushed a button that opened the door. "What do you want with me? And by the way, you're wrong about your not being to blame. If not you, who then? I was a volunteer under your authority, and something bad happened to me. I'm not sure what it was, and I don't think the doctors even know what it was, but it was bad."

Chan took the lead. "We are looking for Richard Wilson, a former Coast Guard officer who stole an aircraft. We know that you fished with Wilson, and suspect you had some other dealings with him. We suspect he is in Austin, and at this juncture you are our only point of contact."

"That scoundrel is in Austin?"

"We suspect he might be. We don't know for sure."

"What makes you suspect he might be, to use your inane phraseology."

"He renewed his passport, and did not apply for any foreign visas. By process of elimination, we concluded that he was USA bound."

"That's it? Buford said, raising his eyebrows. "Pretty thin evidence. Why didn't you just alert immigration and customs and Homeland Security, whatever the hell they are?"

" We did that, sir," Bunch said quickly.

"And so did they get a hit?"

"No sir," Bunch replied.

"So let me summarize what I'm hearing. You are looking for Richard Wilson. And before I go on, let me insert here that Richard Wilson is about as bright as a thousand foot coal mine with no lights on. If he had to have brain surgery, they'd have to have a bloodhound by the table or the surgeon wouldn't find it, and if he should ever leave his brain to science, they would have to mount the entire thing on a microscopic slide.

"But getting back to the job at hand, we think that Wilson might be in Austin, but he has not been seen at any point of entry into the USA. So we should conclude he's not in the USA. And why do you think he *might* be in the USA? Because he renewed his passport. Have I got that right so far?"

"Yes, sir," Bunch acknowledged.

Then to Chan, Parker said, "FBI? Did it not occur to you that you are drawing conclusions that are about as relevant to your search as the can of boneless, skinless sardines I had for breakfast this morning?"

"It's what we have to go on, sir. We can think of no other reason he would come back to the USA than to deal with some problem he's having with you."

"Did it occur to you that he might renew his passport because he lives in a foreign country and needs it to remain there? Or did you consider that on the outside chance that he is coming to the USA, that he is doing so because he is having a class reunion? I believe he attended school at San Diego State.

Did you check the year and the reunion schedule. Or did you consider the fact that Richard Wilson is so stupid that he just decided to renew his passport for no good reason?"

"You have made several valid points, Mr. Parker, but we desperately want to capture this outlaw, and we need to play with the cards we are dealt," Chan advised.

"Does Mr. Bart Knowland know what y'all are up to?"

"Yes, he assigned me to the task," Chan said. "Mr. Bunch got his orders from the Vice Commodore of the Coast Guard."

"It was my privilege to receive a phone call from Mr. Knowland a couple years back. I think he might be smarter than Wilson, but that is only because everybody on earth is."

Chan responded, "We would like to be able to count on your help in our search for Wilson. As we all know, he has evaded capture for two years. We need to bring him to justice."

"Gentlemen, in my considered view, you are barking up the wrong tree. You know what that means? That means the coon is not in the tree that the dog has selected as the tree that the coon is in. In other words I do not think that Wilson is in the USA at all, and if by some longshot chance he is, it is not likely that he is in the great state of Texas, much less Austin. All that said, I pledge my cooperation. As always, I am at the service of anyone who wants to capture that lout. But at this moment I need to get my groceries. I love my boneless, skinless sardines, but I've been livin' on em for a few days now, and it's time to get me some Texas vittles. That means beef, and it means about five or six varieties of chilies, and maybe some grits. Will that be all, gentlemen, or do you need something more out of me?"

Bunch and Chan looked at one another, and neither could think of the right thing to say, even if there was one. Finally Chan said, "We will keep you posted, sir."

"Keep me posted? So that's what you'll do. And how will you do that? Do you plan to telephone me? If so, do you know what my telephone number is? Well, at least I can feel confident that I will be posted. Posted of nothing, since there will be nothing to post. Do you two gov'ment agents have a pursuit and capture plan? Or is this one of those situations where you'll rely on luck and good fortune. It sounds like the latter to me, but now that I'm confident that you will keep me posted, I'll be able to sleep at night. Now if y'all'd be so kind as to get out of my way, I'd like to go down to Central Market and get me some vittles. But while I'm there, you can be confident that I'll be keeping my eyes peeled for the desperado you are trying to apprehend."

"I'll get the car out of the way, Mr. Parker." Chan said. "Let's get the hell out of here," he said quietly to Bunch.

As they drove away, Chan said, "Do you feel a little silly?"

"No, I don't, Charlie. We're on orders to capture Wilson. This is all we have to go on."

"Okay. We'll have to prepare a status report for the guys upstairs. You want to handle that?"

"That's okay, you can do it, Charlie."

CHAPTER TWENTY -NINE

Willy's girlfriend was Angelina Guerrera. She did, indeed, take an instant liking to the tall, sandy haired Wilson. The three of them played low-stakes poker as Willy and Richard swapped stories of their youth. The game folded after a couple of hours and Richard fell asleep on a couch that was in the control room. The next morning he decided it was time to discuss planning with his former classmate.

"*Cuate*, it looks like you'd be able to tell me how to find Buford Parker."

"I could tell you how to find him, and I could take you to wherever he is. I'm wired to find out about anything you want to know."

"Okay, we'll mobilize in a day or two."

"Why not now?"

"In a day or two. I'm still mulling over whether the idea I have in mind is the best way to accomplish my goal."

"And your goal is to get money out of this guy Parker?"

"*Si, Cuate, eso es.*"

"That's my job, *Amigo*. That's what I do for a living. Do you think that the people who lose their bets pay me off with glee and happiness?"

"Never gave it much thought."

"Well, sometimes they need to be encouraged."

"And who does the encouraging?"

"I have hired help. They know how to do some of the things that we educated folks don't. As you know, we go to school to learn the intricacies of life. There are many people in the world who know the intricacies of only one thing about life. The thing they do. They are indispensable to global dynamics because they become far better at their one skill than anyone else. Put another way, people like us who are imaginative and clever are able to see on a broad spectrum, the tasks that need to be accomplished. But we don't know how to accomplish them so we find an expert at that one task and pay him to do the job, *entiendes?*"

"*Si, entiendo.* I still want to give some more thought to the program. I took a huge risk to come here and I don't want to fuck it up."

"I understand what you're saying, but in this case there is no reason to wait. I am so on it that all waiting does is waste time. But you're the boss, *Cuate*, I'll wait for the word from you, my friend."

℃

To his relief, when Buford Parker returned to his home, Bunch and Chan had departed. But Parker did not overlook the reality that he was vulnerable. *Those two idiots not only found me but drove right up to my garage in their automobile,* he thought. *I've got to prepare for the unexpected. I've got to establish my defense against invasion. I thought all I had to worry about was the idiots at that hospital coming to try to take me back. Now I find that Richard Wilson, the great experiment in artificial irrationality, might be around. How that man's eyes stay in their sockets with the vacuum that exists inside his skull is a mystery that would have caused the great German physicist Werner Heisenberg to go nuts-o. Is there a science of nothing? Nothingology? Can you contribute a vacuum to science? But he can fish. He must operate on a DNA map that functions independent of any reasoning. But is that not the most dangerous kind of animal. One that behaves on instinct alone. Yes, I need to raise my defenses. As a minimum, I have to arm myself with my twelve gauge Browning. Be observant –*

of course. If it comes to fisticuffs, I would not prevail. Consequently, I must prepare for a battle of brain power. High intelligence vs. a complete absence of matter – gray or otherwise.

Parker put the grocery bags on the kitchen counter and proceeded to his library, where he kept a small arsenal of hand guns, rifles, and shotguns. *Now here is where the choices become crucial.* The twelve gauge Browning was his first weapon of choice. In addition he had a military issue Colt .45 semiautomatic pistol. He had never developed expertise with it, but that was a last resort if someone was able to get by the shotgun. Buford Parker smiled in the smug way that defined his lifelong attitude toward all of humankind.

୨୦

Wilson's curiosity was so awakened by Willy's certainty of success that he could not refrain from asking for more information.

"How do they do it?"

"There are certain things that I don't know and nobody is allowed to know."

"Can I go? I want to see Parker squirm."

"Hell, no, *Cuate.* These guys are skilled craftsmen. They are like the great master painters, who would never allow anyone to observe their work until it was completed. They are, in fact, masters of their trade. They are master debt collectors."

"If Parker gets word that I'm in town, he'll set booby traps all around his yard, or around wherever he is. I think you are asking too much of your guys, Willy."

"When the time comes, just say the word. The job will be done. I don't know how they do it, but they do. I pay them well. If they need to cross a mine field, they will cross it."

CHAPTER THIRTY

Admiral Gene Skilling, USCG, pressed the intercom for his secretary. "Julie, will you get Bart Knowland on the phone for me?"

"Yes, sir," replied Chief YNS Julia Emerson.

"Mr Knowland, line two, sir," she told him momentarily.

"Admiral, what's up?"

"That's what we need to find out, Bart. I had a strange call from my guy, Commander Bunch, a couple days ago and I can't make heads nor tails of it. Have you had a status report from your Houston agent?"

"No word so far, Gene. What was the strange call?"

"In a nutshell, Bunch accused your guy – correct me if I'm wrong – Chan? He accused Chan of shacking up with a woman who we hoped would be an informant."

"I'm surprised you didn't call right away."

"Well, Bunch also told me that he fainted while he was talking to another of the women we thought could help out."

"Fainted?"

"That's what he said, Bart."

"They're supposed to be working as a team. I wonder why Chan went in alone."

"That's what I asked, and Bunch said he didn't feel so good."

"My god, Gene, it sounds like you and I should have taken on the job ourselves. Pretty hard to believe. I picked Chan because he has a couple awards for valor."

"My commander has done some heroic rescue work. I don't get it either."

"What would you think of telling these two to pack up their things and go home, and you and I can go down to Austin and straighten things out."

"I like the idea, Bart, but I have a four day conference with the chief of Homeland Security starting tomorrow. But I'll tell you what. There's an Admiral Robyn Fritz on assignment in Galveston that we could send up to Austin to meet you."

"I hate to take these guys off the chase, Gene, but the report you got from Bunch does sound flaky."

"When can you get to Austin, Bart?"

"Tomorrow. I'll let you know my flight arrangements."

"Call Robyn directly. I'll have Chief Emerson give you the number."

Knowland had the FBI office travel assistant get him onto a flight to Austin, and asked his secretary to get Admiral Fritz for him. "Line one," she said moments later.

"Admiral Fritz, this is Bart Knowland, executive assistant director or the criminal, cyber, response, and services branch of the FBI. How are you today?"

"Fine, sir, Admiral Skilling told me you would be calling."

From the tenor of the voice, Knowland judged that he was talking to a woman, which surprised him. "Together, Skilling and I decided that you and I should relieve the two men who have been assigned to track and capture Richard Wilson. Did he brief you on that?"

"Yes sir, he did. The case is not new to me. I did some of the planning for the flight to Argentina a couple years ago. I'm looking forward to getting my feet on the ground for this one."

"Well, I don't like the circumstance that brings us to the fray, but it will be a pleasure working with you. I'm glad you know the case. I've been on it for a couple of years, too. As you know, we don't even know that Wilson is in Austin, but maybe we can find out together."

"I'll drive up tomorrow, Bart, if I may call you by your name, and meet you at Austin-Bergstrom. I won't be wearing my uniform. How will we recognize each other?"

"I'll put a sticker on my attache case that says, 'I heart NY.'"

"Love it, Bart. See ya tomorrow."

CHAPTER THIRTY-ONE

When Betty Jane's phone rang, it was Tina. "Guess who I'm dating, BJ."

"How could I ever guess that?"

"Duh. How could you not even guess? It's Ronald Talbot."

"The guy with ED?"

"No more, bud. He's become a pizza lover. We go out for pizza every night."

"Do you ever do the PCB trick?"

"I did it one other time. I told him that I had a medication that would enhance his performance and enjoyment of sex, but did not tell him he was eating cat balls. I think that could have caused a recurrence of the ED. Ronald is really a nice guy, and as you can imagine, he is so, so obliged to me for fixing his problem. This friendship is not going to last, but it's fun for now."

"Why won't it last?"

"Because I like my independence and freedom. Why do you think we live in the USA?"

"Might as well throw liberty and justice into the equation, Tina."

"That, too. I just don't like being tied down. Listen, are we finished with your old pal Buford? I don't see why we didn't take the whole jar when we knew which ones were good. Also, when we first discussed him it sounded like you probably wanted to extract some form of retribution. Is that still on the agenda?

"I don't know. I *have* been thinking about him. I thought I was getting retribution when I moved the *good* sticker to the new jar, but now we don't even know whether the jar I put the sticker on has the pellets with the poison or the brew that is true."

"We could do a test."

"How could we do that, Tina?"

"I'm not sure yet. Let me think about it."

₭

Robyn Fritz spotted the I heart NY sticker as she watched the passengers file by her in the South Terminal. "Hey, Bart," she called.

"Robyn?"

"That's me," she said. They shook hands. "Thanks for meeting me," Bart offered.

Robyn Fritz was a stunning woman, younger than you would expect of an admiral, and taller than you would expect of a woman. She had lightened, streaked hair, dark blue eyes, and a classically handsome face. Her Bermuda shorts and light blouse were not only a perfect contrast to the dark suit that Knowland was wearing, but enhanced her natural beauty. When she chose the outfit, she knew that it would be in contrast to whatever Knowland would be wearing, but she reasoned that the less official they looked, the less attention they would draw.

The moment she hailed him, Knowland deduced why she had dressed that way, and felt remiss in not thinking of it himself. "You're very appropriately dressed for the job at hand," he said. "I did bring along some informal clothes. I'll change at the hotel."

"I'm glad you approve. I just thought that formal attire – or a uniform, in my case, in Austin, especially in the summer, would be like a big target that said 'enforcement squad. So I threw on my 'mudas. What's the plan? Have you reasoned out a strategy yet?"

"No, I thought we could discuss it over lunch. Shall we find a place here?"

"We could, I guess. Actually, I'm partial to Burger King."

"Well, I'll be damned. So am I."

On the way to their hotel they found a BK, coincidentally the Burger King that served as the entrance to Willy Lopez's cave, and ordered a whopper each. Both asked for heavy pickle. "We seem to have similar tastes," Robyn commented.

Knowland smiled. "I wonder if we have similar thoughts about how to proceed."

"I have no thoughts about how to proceed. I'm hoping you do."

"To be honest, I don't either. What we know is that the guy who apparently was planning to kill Wilson lives here in Austin. We *think* Wilson might be either in the US now, or is planning a trip here. And we *think* the reason he would come here is to see Parker. We don't even know why."

"Thin. Thin. Maybe we shouldn't have come down so hard on the two guys who were on it."

"They weren't just baffled. Their behavior was questionable."

"That's what Gene told me."

"There are also three women that were out at Parker's place when our two guys went out there to check out Parker. They followed them to a warehouse sized bar and talked to them briefly there, and then followed one of them out to her house. That's where things get a little blurred."

"Maybe we should start there."

Knowland furrowed his brow. "There?"

"At the woman's house. The place where things got blurred."

"That's not a bad idea. Maybe she'd give us her side of the story."

"If we assume that she works, probably the best time to go would be around six."

"Sounds right, Robyn. Let's check into the hotel. I might nap for awhile. We'll head over at six. Her name is Betty Jane Griffin. I have the address. We can meet in the hotel lobby at, say, five, five-thirty?"

"Sounds good to me. Five-thirty. Maybe you should leave the suit in your room."

℘

They found Betty Jane's house, and went up to the front door together. They rang and listened to Betty Jane's footsteps approach the door. "Yes?" she said.

"I'm Robyn Fritz of the US Coast Guard. This is Bart Knowland of the FBI. As you know, I'm sure, we're looking for Ricardo Wilson. Could we come in and ask you a few questions?"

"A few. I'm tired of hearing about Wilson. I don't know the man."

They sat in a front room area with a nice view of the Colorado River in the distance. "Lovely house," Robyn said.

"What are the questions?"

Knowland asked, "Did one of my agents, a Michael Chan, visit a few nights ago to ask some questions?"

"Yes."

"Did he spend the night?"

"Yes."

"Why did he spend the night?"

"Did you say he was your agent?"

"Yes."

"Then ask him."

"I'm asking you."

"I am aware of that. That's why I said ask him. He's your agent. I'm just a woman who you must think knew this Wilson, but I do not and never did."

133

"We would like to ascertain why Chan spent the night here."

"Ask him."

"Can you help us out here, Ms. Griffin?"

"I doubt it, but I'll try."

"Then let's start with why did Chan spend the night here."

"You can start there, but so far it has not worked out very well as a starting point."

Robyn then asked, "Was Commander Bunch with him?"

"No."

"He wasn't?"

"No. He wasn't."

"Do you know who I'm talking about?"

"Yes, the guy who fainted over at the Hookem House."

"He did faint?"

"Yes."

"Any idea what caused him to faint?"

"No."

"He told our Vice Commodore that he hit his chin while falling. Does that match up with what you saw happen?"

"I did not notice that part, but when he finally came around he was rubbing his chin."

"Rubbing his chin?"

"May I ask you something at this point?"

"Of course," Robyn and Bart said pretty much in unison.

"When I tell you something you always repeat it as a question. Is that an interrogation technique?"

Robyn and Bart looked at each other sheepishly. Finally Robyn said, "We know that Mr. Chan spent the night here and that Mr. Bunch lost consciousness on the job. Neither of those behaviors were appropriate to their assignments. We must somehow ferret out why this happened, and you are the only one we know of who might be able to shed some light on that situation. We are senior to both men and are replacing them, hopefully to do a better job. So far as I can tell, their peculiar sagas may be the result of getting stonewalled, the way you're stonewalling us. Now I think you owe us some cooperation."

"Well, Ms. Fritz. That's where you're wrong. I don't owe you shit."

ৎ৶

Paula had been staying in a motel for four days and was starting to wonder what she was doing. Initially, she was doing Karole the favor of trying to locate Richard. Although she did not know where Richard was, she had talked to him on the telephone, and he seemed content to lay low and to need nothing from her. Meanwhile, she hadn't heard word one from Karole. *What am even doing here,* she thought. *It would give me a huge satisfaction to lay another bolo onto Buford Parker, but the chances of getting that opportunity seem remote. Maybe I should call Betty Jane and see what she's up to.* She punched in Betty Jane's number and when BJ picked up the phone there was no missing the fact that she was steamed about something.

"Whoa, BJ. I am so very sorry to invade your space. It sounds like whatever is in your life right now is not good."

"Oh, Paula. I'm sorry. But you're right. The US Coast Guard and FBI just left. My god. They said they were the supervisors of the two guys who showed up at the Hookem House. But they were *so* tedious and inane. Have you talked to Tina?"

"No, I haven't talked to anyone. I'm beginning to wonder what I'm doing here."

"Well, after we left the Hookem House, Michael Chan showed up at my house to ask some questions. I thought it would be fun to distract him a little and have some fun myself. Long story short, I gave him one of the PCBs that we took away from Parker. Chan was indeed distracted. We spent the night together, and somehow his boss found out and these two dolts showed up wanting to know why Chan spent the night.

135

One was a woman from the Coast Guard. She said I *owed* it to them to cooperate. I politely told them that I did not agree."

"Poor you. How was the session with Chan."

"Memorable, thanks."

"Do you have any plans to pursue any aspect of the Buford Parker situation?"

"That's up in the air, Paula. Tina is trying to figure out some way to test the testes to determine which are good and which are bad. I did a chemical analysis of one that I know is a good one, and came up with a compound that is not described anywhere. Oh my gosh, now that I tell you that, I realize that it might be possible to separate the two different batches by doing a spectral analysis of each batch. All I'd have to do is keep track of the batches I tested. There should be some that look one way, and some that look another way. If we could get back in there and get all of them I might be able to separate them into good and bad, even if I didn't know how to duplicate the organic compound. God, I'm glad you called. If I hadn't started talking about it, I probably wouldn't have figured that out."

"Betty Jane, you're an angel. Here I catch you at a bad time and you make me feel good about it. Should I just head back up to Omaha, or is there something else I can do down here?"

"Don't go, Paula. If we go back to Parker's place, we might need you. You're the enforcer."

"You are sweeter'n candy, Betty Jane."

&

As soon as they had said good-bye, Betty Jane punched up Tina on her phone. Tina saw who was calling and said, "What's up?"

"One, the FBI and Coast Guard sent their big guns over to squeeze me for why Chan spent the night. But the best news is that right after they left, Paula called and during our conversation, it came to me that if we can get our hands on all the marbles, good and bad, I can just run them through the spectrograph and I'll get two different pictures. I already know what a good one looks like. It will be a lead pipe cinch." She went on to apprise Tina of the visit by the investigator team, and finally said. "So what do you think? Think we can snag all the marbles somehow?"

"I'm not sure. Let me think about it."

"Do you know that's exactly what you said last time we rang off?"

"No. But thinking about stuff is something I do well. Your idea to go and get 'em is great. I'll see if I can come up with a strategy. After all, we did it once. Why can't we do it again?"

CHAPTER THIRTY-TWO

Admiral Robyn Fritz looked at Knowland. "That didn't go so well."

"It did not," Bart agreed. "What's left? Parker? Do you think we should go out to his place and talk to him?"

"It's about all we've got at this point."

"Now, or tomorrow?"

"Tomorrow."

"Well, Robyn, maybe we should have dinner together."

"I guess we could do that. Burger King?"

"No, let's find some quiet restaurant near our hotel."

"Sounds good. I'll meet you in the lobby in an hour. By the way, did you send Mr. Chan home?"

"Didn't I tell you?"

"What?"

"When I told him that I was going to take over his assignment, he quit. Without any hesitation at all, he just told me he was going to resign and said he'd make it official with a letter to headquarters. Chan quit. I don't know where he is now or what his future plans are."

"Jesus, Bart. I was thinking that Betty Jane was right. We should ask Chan why he spent the night out there."

"We could call his cell, but I've tried him a couple times to try to talk him out of resigning. He's not answering."

&

This time, Tina really did think over what she had promised. She knew they had to steal the PCBs, but could not devise a plan to get them out of the house. In fact she could not think of any excuse that would get them into the house. The only thing she could come up with was to go out to Parker's place and snoop around. Maybe they'd get lucky again and he wouldn't be there or would be napping. And there was Paula. The ace in the hole. If worst came to worst she could do her thing. Tina and Betty Jane agreed to meet at the Hookem House the following day at noon. When Betty Jane called Paula to tell her the plan, Paula was elated.

"Nothin' I'd enjoy more than planting another one in that guy's chops," she exclaimed.

℮

Even after one day, Buford Parker was getting tired of packing his shotgun and military .45 around with him everywhere he went. He decided that if he left the pistol near the front door and the shotgun in his living room that he would have ample time to prepare himself for anything that might ensue. Just to play it safe, he put another loaded shotgun in his garage.

℮

Robyn and Bart ordered pasta dishes and Chianti at Numero 28 restaurant. The menu was not exactly what Robyn had in mind, but better than California cuisine with minuscule servings designed more for the eye than the palate. The admiral had reached a point in her career where respect was almost always the rule, and rude, bullying treatment was essentially absent. The insulting experience with Betty Jane made her crave a juicy steak or perhaps a rack of lamb, but the meaty pasta would have to suffice. Bart was happy to order linguini with Alfredo sauce and clams.

"We're not doing any better than Beavis and Butthead," Robyn noted after the wine was poured.

"I assume you're referring to Chan and Bunch. And you're right. We need to get creative."

"Bart, there's nothing to create. We have to visit Parker. He's the only lead we have besides the stubborn young lady we just visited."

"What do you have in mind?"

"We'll just have to go out there and see what we can see."

"Seems a little vague, but we can try it, I guess. Parker does not like Wilson. That was clear from the report that your staffers wrote after the Argentina trip. He might be willing to help once he knows what we're after. Chan told me that he has a several acre spread. What would you think about interviewing Parker yourself while I have a look around the property?"

"Can't think of what good looking around the property would do, but if that's what you want, go for it. You don't think he's got Wilson caged out there, do you?"

"I don't think anything. I just think it would be good to get the lay of the land. It won't take long. I'll join you after I've checked out the place."

℘

Parker saw the car arrive in plenty of time to grab his shotgun and position himself near a window that looked out onto the driveway and turnaround loop. He saw two individuals emerge from the car, and watched while one approached the door and the other went off toward the area where Frenzy the Pampas Cat had once been kept.

Holy Christ. What a beautiful woman, Parker thought. *I could not possibly shoot a specimen like that if my life depended on it. Oh lordie, lordie, she is going to come right up here to m'door. Could she be from the hospital? No. I'd know it if she was from the hospital. She must be another fool who thinks I know where Wilson is.*

Parker moved his two weapons to an inconspicuous corner behind a highboy chest of drawers and went to the front door as the bell rang.

"Mr. Parker?"

"At your service, ma'am. What can I do for you?"

Robyn, who was a couple of inches taller than Parker, said, "May I come in?"

"Honey you may. You may. What can I offer you?"

"Nothing, thank you."

"Coffee? I just brewed up a pot. How about a cup of coffee?"

"Well, coffee would be nice. Thank you."

Buford Parker knew he had to get a Pampas Cat ball into the coffee, but he did not know how to go about it. Finally he asked, "Sugar?"

"Yes, please. About a teaspoon."

Hot damn, that'll do it. Between the coffee and sugar, she'll never taste a thing. I'd better have a little myself, just to make sure I don't fail her. Buford quickly grabbed a jar from the pantry and minced one ball with a sharp cleaver. He put it into two cups of coffee and added sugar to one of them.

"Here you go, honey," he said. "Now, what can I do for you?" Parker tasted his coffee. *Not too bad,* he thought. *She'll never notice – especially with the sugar. Hot damn. Did I die? Is this heaven, or what?*

&ʊ

Bart toured through the yard and inspected the interior of several outbuildings that were on the property. The landscaping and buildings were in disrepair and from all appearances had been neglected for some time. *This guy has a beautiful piece of property and doesn't take care of it,* Bart thought. He continued looking around, not really certain what he was looking for. After fifteen minutes of finding nothing, he heard a muffled scream from inside the house. Bart ran to the front door and rang the bell. No answer. He tried to open it but couldn't. It was locked. During his yard tour, he had spotted a side door, so he ran to it and found it unlocked. Noises that defied any description were coming from the front room. *God, they're fighting,* he thought.

When Bart Knowland got to the front room, the scene he found was so extremely remote from anything that he could possibly ever have imagined that he stood for several seconds, mouth agape, looking. The beautiful Robyn Fritz was engaged in a sexual frenzy with the roly poly man that was supposed to be the bait for Richard Wilson.

"Robyn. Robyn. What's going on? Robyn. What the fuck? Robyn."

"Beat it, Bart. What's it look like? I'm fucking this little fat man. Get the hell out."

"Oooohh, oh, my," Bart heard Parker groan. "Ooohhh."

Meanwhile Robyn was sounding more like a spring robin than the staid woman Bart had eaten dinner with the night before. Bart tried to separate them but could not.

"Get the fuck away," Robyn commanded. Finally, Bart threw a punch at Buford's jaw that connected. Buford went limp. In no time flat, Robyn had Bart's pants off and although it took her a minute or two to get him to acquiesce, he, in complete disbelief of what he was doing or what was happening, was having sex with Robyn. A generous estimate would be that it lasted for two or three minutes, at which time Bart did not know what to do. Robyn was still ravenous, but he was feeling enormous guilt along with extreme sense of wonder about what had just happened.

Now, Robyn went back to Parker and revived him, and within moments they were at it again. Bart, flummoxed, went into the bathroom and looked at himself in the mirror. He looked ten years older than he had that very morning. *Good lord. What is going on here,* he thought. *First things first, I've got to get my pants on.* He got back to the living room in time to see a Buick LeSabre coming down the driveway. He could tell that there were three people inside the car, but as yet could not tell who they were. They appeared to be women. *Where are my god damn pants?* He found them under Parker and Robyn and managed to pull them loose. When he looked out of the window, he could see that the women were still in the car. Now he could see that the driver was Betty Jane. *What in god's name is she doing out here? And with two other women? They must be the ones that Chan followed to that cowboy bar.* As he struggled to get into his pants, he felt relieved that the women had not yet emerged from the car. *What to do?* he thought. Exhausted, he fell into an overstuffed chair.

&

As Betty Jane, Tina, and Paula approached Parker's house they stopped the car about three hundred feet before his driveway.

"I'll get out and scout the scene, Tina said from the back seat."

When she returned to the car she told them that she could see a vehicle parked in the turnaround near the front door. She told them it looked like a brown Ford Focus.

"Isn't that the car that those guys have – the guys who've been snooping around looking for Wilson?" Paula wondered aloud.

"Yep, I wonder what those clowns are doing here," Tina said.

"Me too," Betty Jane added. Snooping is right. Those are the nosiest people I've ever seen in my life."

"Let's go find out," Paula urged.

The other two were uncertain.

"Come on," Paula said again.

Finally, Betty Jane said, "I agree. Let's go."

Betty Jane slid the lever into drive and slowly cruised down the driveway toward the house. She stopped behind the Focus and all three sat in the car silently, each wondering what was next. Paula got out. "I'm going in," she said. "You guys do what you want, but I'm going in the side door. The guy is probably guarding the front door with an arsenal of booby traps and firearms."

Tina and Betty Jane looked at each other. Finally, Tina said, "Paula, if the coast is clear, open the front door."

Paula found the side door open and went inside. Right away, she heard strange noises coming from the front room. She made her way toward the sounds and stopped short when she saw a naked butt in motion before her. A man she did not recognize was sitting in a chair looking dazed, his pants neither zipped or buttoned, looking on. Upon closer inspection of the naked butt she saw that there were two of them in wild sexual ebullience. One was Buford Parker. Quickly she groped for her phone and snapped off two shots before Bart was out of the chair and grappling for the cell phone. That lasted three seconds. Paula's first uppercut hit him squarely in the chin and he hit the floor like George Foreman hit the canvas in the "Rumble in the Jungle."

Paula went to the pantry and put the six mason jars into a Trader Joe's bag she found there, then stopped in the front room to snap three more photos. Robyn and Buford were still fucking their brains out and did not notice. Neither did Bart Knowland who was out like Foreman on the living room floor.

When Paula opened the front door, Betty Jane and Tina saw it and started to get out of the car. Paula signaled them to stay put and arrived at the passenger side door and got in with the Trader Joe's bag.

"Got 'em," she said.

"Got what? You got the PCBs?" Betty Jane shouted.

"Yep. Got 'em. I also got these."

She got out her phone and showed them the five photographs she'd taken.

"Who are these people?" Tina inquired. "Other than Buford."

"Betty Jane recognized all of them. "Those are the two that showed up at my place to ask about Chan. They're from the FBI and the Coast Guard. "Why is that guy on the floor? You clocked him didn't you, Paula. You cold cocked him, you rascal. How do you do it?"

"Let's roll," Tina said. "We've got what we came for. That scene in there is not going to last forever. Hopefully, they won't even remember that we were there."

CHAPTER THIRTY-THREE

The following day was Saturday and Betty Jane took the bagful of sample jars to the laboratory where she worked. As expected, when she ran specimens from each of the six jars through the spectrometer, she found that the contents of three of the jars had a spike similar to the one she had found in her previous test. The spike was absent from the samples from the other three jars. She put sticky labels on all six jars, three saying *good,* and three with a skull and crossbones carefully scribed onto the label. *What a treasure. Even the toxic ones might come in handy, who knows? Meanwhile, there's a few other questions that I need the answers to.*

She took out her phone and pressed quick dial for Michael Chan. As she was wondering whether he would answer, he did.

"Hi, Betty Jane. This is a pleasant surprise."

"I'm glad it is. Did you get fired or something?"

"No, I quit. I thought of phoning you, but to be honest I did not really know where we stood with each other."

"Why did you quit?"

"My boss is Bart Knowland. I think Bunch told him I spent the night with you, and at that point he decided that he might be a better candidate to do my assigned task than I was."

"If you would come over to my place, I could enlighten you on some things. In fact I have a story to tell that will probably warm the cockles of your heart."

"Why don't we meet for dinner?"

"Come on over Michael. I'll put together something tasty."

"Now?"

"If you're not doing anything."

"I'm not. I spent yesterday and this morning trying to figure out where to go from here. I'm suddenly jobless."

"I'm sure you'll have an opportunity to change that if you decide you want to. Come on over."

An hour later, Michael Chan arrived at Betty Jane's door clearly having just showered. Betty Jane wasn't sure where to start. She had to explain that Pampas Cat balls, PCBs, were a strong aphrodisiac and that she had slipped him half of one when he last visited. She also needed to tell him about their foray out to the ranch the previous day.

"How about a beer?" she said. "I've got so much to tell you that we'll probably go through three each before I'm done."

"I'll get them," Chan said. He went to the fridge, extracted a couple of Coors, and popped them open. "Sounds more than intriguing."

For an hour and a half, and the predicted three beers, Betty Jane explained the story of Buford Parker, her own research to find the Pampas Cat pheromone, and the incredible powers of the balls. She told him that that was what had triggered their wonderful night the previous week. And finally she told him that she now had the entire harvest from Argentina.

During the telling of the tale, Chan retrieved fresh beers as they were emptied, but never once asked a question or said a word. His attention was rapt, and his facial expression evidenced his awe. At the end of the story he simply said, "I don't know what to say. I have seen just enough to know that your unlikely – even unbelievable – story must be true. You know you have a treasure that endangers you if it were to become known that you have it."

"I do know that. I am going to divide it up with Tina and Paula. I'm not sure Paula wants any, but I'll offer it."

"Warn them that the powers of the PCB and their possession present a hazard, or I should say a real danger. You probably know that the quest for a universal aphrodisiac is legendary throughout history. People would kill to get what you have."

"I do know that. I value your concern, and I will be careful. I hope I can trust that your lips are sealed."

"Clearly."

"There is one more thing," she said, and showed Chan the five photos that Paula had texted to her.

"Good god. What in the hell are these? I see Knowland, and I see Parker. I don't know the woman. My lord, what is going on?"

Betty Jane told the story that went with the pictures. It took another half hour and another beer. "These will explain my comment that you probably could get your job back if you were to choose to."

"I've given that a lot of thought. Even without knowing what you just told me, I am not going back, even if they beg me."

"What are you going to do?"

"As I said, I'm a day and a half into that and haven't found an answer. It'll come. No hurry."

"I promised you a dinner, Michael. I hope you like Kung Pao chicken."

"Let's go out. My treat."

"You don't like Kung Pao chicken?"

"I'd rather have barbecued back ribs. They serve em at a place a block from here."

"I know. I love em."

CHAPTER THIRTY-FOUR

Paula went through her usual checklist before calling someone. Will it be invasive to their privacy? To their time? Too personal? She could not wait to tell Richard about her coup while making what was only meant to be an exploratory trip out to Buford Parker's place. Whenever she had called him he seemed happy to talk to her, so she punched in his number.

"Hi Paula. What's up?"

"I just got back from Buford's ranch, and you won't believe all that happened out there. Got a minute – or I should say do you have a half hour. It's a long story."

"I've got time, Paula. What happened?"

Paula gave Richard a blow by blow recounting of all that had transpired, describing her knock out punch with great relish and in minute detail. She concluded by saying that BJ now had all the jars of PCBs from Buford's pantry, and would test them to separate the good ones from the toxic ones. "Do you want some, Richard?" she asked.

"No. All the time I was collecting them I kept wondering if I should keep any and I always decided no. Ingrid tried one and said one was enough."

"Okay, Richard. Just checkin'."

"As always, you're a sweetheart, Paula. Thanks."

"There's one other thing I wanted to talk to you about."

"Shoot."

"I have an idea that you might like to consider."

"What is it."

149

Paula described a plan to Richard that she had mused over during the time she was alone in the motel. "What do you think?" she said at the end.

"I like it. I have some stuff to take care of first, but when that's finished, I'll let you know."

"Anything I can help with?"

"Nope. But thanks. What I'm doing won't take long, so I'll be calling you soon. I'll try to give you a day's notice."

"I'll be ready, Richard."

৪১

When it occurred to Paula that she should call Karole, she did not need to go through her decision tree about whether it was the right thing to do. *Good lord, she sent me down here to look for Richard, and I haven't even told her that I talked to him on the telephone. It's going to break her heart when I tell her that Richard is on a one-track mission to find Buford Parker, but I have to tell her.*

Paula punched the Karole call button.

"Hey, Paula. Where are you?"

"Still in Austin. How are things with you?"

"Have you found Richard?"

Here goes a tantrum, thought Paula before she spoke. "I don't know where he is exactly, but he *is* in Austin. I talked to him on the phone."

"How about that? So did I," Karole said.

"You did?"

"Yeah. He doesn't want to see me. I was dreamin', sweetie. He's here to catch Parker. That's all. I cried for awhile, but that's now water under the bridge."

"What's that mean?"

"That means I have a new boyfriend. Josh White. I've known him for years, but never let him get close. I used my magic morsel on him and taught him a few lessons along the way. You might say we're an item now."

"Good for you, babe. I love it. I can't see being here more than another couple days. When I get home I'll call. Maybe we can get together again."

"Do that. I've got a lot of things to tell you."

"Hey babe, I can't say for sure, 'cause I don't know what you have to tell me, but I'm betting that what I have to tell you is a tsunami compared to your ripple. It's not a contest or anything. Just guessin'."

"We'll see. Gimme a call when you get home."

CHAPTER THIRTY-FIVE

Betty Jane Griffin and Michael Chan ate six ribs each and put about that many into a bag to take back with them. As they were walking back toward BJ's house, she said, "We have some unfinished business to talk over. Do you have time to come in for a nightcap?"

"I have time, Betty Jane. I have time. Remember I'm jobless at the moment."

They mounted the steps to her house. Michael opened the door to let Betty Jane in. "I have a hunch I know what's on your mind," Michael said.

"Of course you do. Any two people who have had a night like we did have something to talk over. Now you know what happened the other night. We managed to get through dinner without talking about it, but we were helped along by the closeness of the tables. It was a good thing not to talk about at the restaurant."

"Is it a good thing to talk about now?" Michael asked.

"Not only good, but required. When I invited you over, were you just curious, or did get a little bit of that feeling of excitement that happens when you hope that something will happen and then it does."

"I couldn't have said it that way, but yes, I got that feeling."

"Now if we decided that you should spend the night here tonight, would you want me to get out one of my magic morsels so we could have a re-run of the other night?"

"No. It was a nice little ice breaker, but I would say no."

"That's a really good answer. I'm glad you said that. I am going to suggest you stay."

"Maybe I should stay a few nights, so we could iron out anything that might need ironing."

"Maybe so. How did you get the scar on your cheek?"

"It was lain upon me by a cat." Michael answered. "It was a black cat – a cat by the name of Midnight. He was not mine, but was owned by a friend. My friend offered to kill that cat after it had put his claw through my face, but I told him to treat the cat well, that the cat had not intended to harm me. The night before it happened, I had a fortune cookie that said, 'You will have a feline encounter.'"

"Michael, you are a story teller. I like that."

"It doesn't match up to the story you told me before we left for dinner."

"Few if any ever will. I have to believe there is more to come, but we don't yet know how it will end."

"Maybe we should look in a fortune cookie."

"Maybe we should go to bed."

CHAPTER THIRTY-SIX

Toward the end of the second hour with ADM Robyn Fritz, Buford Parker passed out. All the while Bart Knowland had been looking on from an overstuffed chair. He was disheveled from his two minute stint with the admiral, and in fact had still not tucked in his shirt and buttoned up his pants. That worked out nicely, because Robyn was not finished. By this time, Bart, in spite of a nice wife and children in Washington, DC, had decided that his first session with the incredibly alluring Robyn Fritz had not been all that it could have been. During the next hour and a half, he would make up for that. Robyn was, by now, slowing down, and it made the encounter tender, yet nevertheless electrifying.

Buford was motionless on the floor, but not unconscious. He had now, he thought, on seven different occasions consumed one entire, or a half, of a Pampas Cat testicle. Each time, at the conclusion it was harder for him to regain his physical capabilities. Now he struggled to move and found it nearly impossible. Each effort produced a slight movement response which, of course, went unnoticed by the new romancers above him. Bart Knowland was fully recovered from his earlier bout with guilt and uncertainty, and was balling away with reckless abandon. The admiral was loving every second and kept him going by shouting out encouraging instructions.

"Harder, harder. Ride em cowboy. That's it, baby, don't stop," and so on and so on. Eventually, both government personnel ran out of juice and fell asleep side by side on the couch. Robyn's body was every bit as perfect as her sculpted face, and the way they were positioned on the couch would have made a fine gallery exhibit were it a painting.

Another hour passed and Knowland stirred. It appeared to him that Robyn was dead. He trepidatiously put his hand on her breast. It was warm and gently undulating as she breathed.

His feeling of guilt, combined with deep curiosity returned. *I have not only sinned, but have broken every rule and ethic of government service. What am I doing, and what happened? Last night we had dinner together and there was no hint that anything like this was on the horizon. Even more strange, her first choice was Parker. That little fat man is about as sexy as a duck. There has to be more here than meets the eye.*

Bart looked at Robyn. *Jesus, what a body. That was the weirdest thing that's ever happened. Well, I guess she just decided it was a good time to have sex. Still can't figure out why she went for Parker first.*

"Hey," she said, rolling over and sitting up slightly. "That was pretty amazing." She looked at Parker, motionless on the floor, naked. "What's the little fat man doing?"

"You were having sex and he passed out."

"No I wasn't, silly, I was having sex with you. You were great, by the way. I don't know what came over me. Whatever it was, I hope it comes over me again. Do you suppose it means I'm really healthy?

"I think that's probably it, Robyn."

Robyn was lying next to Knowland, still naked. He looked at her amazing body and felt himself stiffen up again. *Oh no, this has got to stop,* he thought. But it didn't. Robyn saw what was happening and moved on top of him. It did not last long, but it was accomplished in full harmonics. They fell asleep again and slept for four hours.

This time Robyn awakened first and was in a daze, not sure where she was or what was happening. She noted to her surprise that everyone in the room was naked, including her.

What goes on here? she thought. Slowly, it started coming back to her. *I had sex with these men. Both of them. Why in the world would I do that? Especially the little fat guy, but same thing with Bart.*

Bart was, himself beginning to stir next to her. *Why would I have sex with Bart? Why would he have sex with me? He's married. Last night we were talking about his kids.* Realizing that she was naked to the bone and Bart was wakening, Robyn grabbed her clothes and started to put them on as quickly as she could.

She was buttoning up her blouse when Bart appeared to regain full consciousness. Bart looked bewildered. "Good god, we made love, didn't we?" he said.

"We sure did."

"I'm sorry, Robyn, I don't know what came over me."

"Don't be sorry. It was a hell of a ride. I just don't know what spurred it."

"I sure as hell can't help you there. All I know is that it was foolhardy – at least on my part."

"On both of our parts, Bart. We're supposed to be on a mission here. Your wife won't mind, I hope."

"Uh, Robyn, were you thinking of telling her?"

"Obviously not. That was a joke."

"We are not going to say a word about this to anyone."

"That seems prudent."

Not until that moment did Bart Knowland piece together the likely reality that the same thing must have been afoot in Michael Chan's indiscretion. What that might have been was the great mystery, but there was more than coincidence involved. To Robyn he said, "I need to apologize to Chan. I need to let him know I understand that somehow control and judgment suddenly disappeared. But why? And how do I tell him? Do I tell him that I was involved in a similar drama? I don't know how I'll do it, but I must get back to him and encourage him to reconsider his resignation. The Bureau needs that guy. He's a hero – one of our most decorated agents. We may never know what happened to us, but it's like someone slipped us an aphrodisiac. I bet the same thing happened to him. I have to figure out what to say to him."

"I agree, Bart. Not only is it something that you need to do, you're the one who needs to figure out how to do it. Maybe you should put your clothes on first."

"Good plan. We should get the hell out of here."

"Can we stop for some food somewhere? I'm famished."

"Burger King," Bart said. "Maybe you can help me figure out what to say to Michael Chan."

They stopped at the BK, where around three hundred feet from them, Willy and Richard were planning their strategy in Willy's subterranean communications center.

ᘓᑎ

Betty Jane and Chan, both feeling the euphoria of a new romance had just poured themselves small snifters of Grand Marnier when Chan's phone rang. He looked at it and saw that it was Bart Knowland.

"Shall I answer it?" Chan asked Betty Jane.

"Probably should."

"It helps that I know some stuff about Bart that he does not know that I know."

Michael swiped his phone. "Good evening, Bart."

"Hello, Michael. Rather than say how are you or any other small talk remark that would put off my reason for calling, I want to ask you to reconsider your resignation. We want you back. No critical reports would be written. In fact we would construct a narrative that would present you in a good light for this investigation."

"Thanks, Bart. I had a hunch that this might happen, so I gave it some serious thought. The answer is no."

"No?"

"Yes. No."

"Would it be out of line for me to ask why?"

157

"No, not out of line. And I don't mind telling you. At the time I told you I quit, I did it indignantly, and doing so – by that I mean resigning – gave me a sense of relief and freedom that I have not experienced for a long, long, time. My work has been exciting, at times dangerous, and almost always rewarding. But it has also been a stressful adventure from dawn to dusk. That I might leave home in the morning and not return at night has not entered into my thinking in the past, but I have begun to feel as if I am missing an important aspect of life by not having to consider anything other than what works for me."

"Well, Chan, I know what you are saying means something to you, but it's a little bit cryptic to me."

"Consider this, Bart. I know that you have a wife and a couple of kids. Now, I think that I could feel completely confident that in any endeavor that the job might confront you with, that before you acted you would consider what it would mean to your loved ones. I suspect that throughout your career you have acted responsibly and have proceeded with your tasks ethically and carefully. I have never had to do that, and I think that not having to factor in those parameters represents a flaw in my life. A hole in my life experience, if you can understand that."

As he spoke, Chan looked at Betty Jane. Her eyes were teary, but she was pumping her fist, knowing that Bart Knowland had to be squirming as he heard Michael's words. She also knew that the words were sincere – that she had aroused in him the sense of responsibility that had evolved into not only the words but the paradigm shift in his attitude that they described.

"Yes, Michael, there is ample merit in your motive, and I appreciate your confidence in me. If you're absolutely sure, go ahead and send in your letter. I'll approve it.

CHAPTER THIRTY-SEVEN

Richard was antsy, and Willy knew it.

"Hey, *Cuate*, when are you going to do something?"

"I know. I need to mobilize."

"No, *amigo*, you don't mobilize. I do."

"I think I should go myself. It's my problem."

"I keep telling you, it's not a problem. I just send one of my guys. I'm going to send my best guy."

"Okay. If you insist. But make sure he doesn't hurt Parker."

"We might have to hurt him."

"Whatever you do, don't kill him."

"We don't kill people, *Cuate*."

"Who is the guy you are going to send?"

"His name is Guido. Guido Jones."

"Guido Jones?"

"That's the guy. He's good."

"Have you instructed him yet?"

"No. Not yet."

"Can I participate in the instructions?"

"It's your deal man. 'Course you can. You're the main guy. You just don't go with Guido. Understand?"

"Okay. If Guido gets the mil out of the guy, you get part."

"I know that man. So does Guido."

"What's your fee?"

"We each get twenty percent. Two hundred large, each."

Richard's surprise showed on his face. The fee had not previously been discussed, and Richard had thought the

159

remuneration would be his gift. He also had a smaller number in mind. Nevertheless, as he contemplated the service that was being offered he had to concede that the fee was probably reasonable. Finally he said, "Okay. Do you want me sign anything?"

"No." Willy's intonation descended several notes on the scale, as though Richard should know that an oral contract was binding – especially with a close friend.

Willy added, "Tomorrow is settle up day. I'll be busy and Guido will be busier. So day after tomorrow is our day. Sound okay, so far?"

"Yeah, whatever you say, Willy. It sounds like you've got this thing pretty well planned out already."

"Sort of. I know where your guy Parker lives, and I know what day Guido is going to go out there. But Guido will be here tomorrow night. We balance the things up every Tuesday. Some guys do it on Monday. Most probably do it that way, but we do it on Tuesday. It's just a decision. We do it on Tuesday. Another guy or two will be here. Collectors, you know? I want you to wait in the bedroom, while they're here; but I'll ask Guido to stay. We can talk then."

ॐ

The next evening a buzzer indicated that all of the collectors were assembled at the Burger King. Willy pressed a button that activated the keypad that the visitors would use to gain entry.

"Get in the bedroom, *amigo*. We'll do the books and then I'll call to you. It'll take an hour. Maybe more, but not much. You got something to keep you busy for an hour or so?"

"Yeah, I'm reading a book. *The Oncorhynchus Affair*. Pretty good book."

"Okay. See you in a few."

An hour and twenty minutes passed and Richard heard Willy call him to come out.

"Hey, *Cuate*, this is Guido." Guido looked like his name should be Guido and that he should be in some kind of business that required that he make demands of people.

"Guido, this is *Cuate*. *Cuate* and I went to school together when we were kids."

Guido nodded. "What's up?"

Willy said, "Buford Parker owes my friend, *Cuate*, a million bucks. It doesn't look like he's going to come across and I want you to go out to his place and collect the money. It is a little more complex than the usual collection, because the guy doesn't think he is ever going to have to pay. It's not like he just lost the bet. He entered into a contract with Rico – that's *Cuate's* real name – and never paid. So your job is not only to get the money, but to remind Mr. Parker why he is in debt. Because of the complex nature of the job, the collection premium will be twenty percent instead of the standard two and a half."

When Richard heard that he lurched in his chair, but said nothing. Guido smiled.

"I've heard of that guy," Guido said.

"How's that?" Willy asked.

"Long story. I had a friend, or let's say an acquaintance, named Francisco Salsipuedes. Sal, we used to call him. This guy we're talking about, Parker, Sal was about to kill him at one time. I'm pretty sure the guy didn't even know it. Sal was representing some people in an apartment that Parker owned, but someone bought the apartment away from Parker and tore it down. It saved Parker's life. Parker probably doesn't even know it. Anyway, that all happened many years ago. I just remember it because I knew Sal. Sal's dead now."

"So what's the plan? Is there anything I need to know. I don't think the guy has a mil in the desk drawer. What's the plan?"

Willy then surprised both of them by telling Guido the name of Parker's bank and the numbers of two of his bank accounts that had more than enough money in them to cover the one million. He even had a couple of Parker's checkbooks. "All you have to do is have him make out a check to yourself. Then you give him this." Willy passed a receipt to Wilson that indicated that the payment settled the account for the Pampas Cat research. "That's the job. I'll leave the details of how to get it done to you, Guido. *Cuate* asked to be involved in the planning, so now is the time, *Cuate*."

"I can't think of anything you didn't already think of," Richard said. "But, I'll mention a couple things you should know. One, Parker is a slick talker. He'll give you a line of shit that will sound so true that you might believe that cozying up to him might make more sense than collecting the money. The other thing is that he also has a violent side. I think he knows that I'm around. I got that from a friend I know from an encounter that I had with Parker in Argentina. It wouldn't surprise me if he is armed and dangerous, to use those cliché words that are always in police warnings."

"I am also armed and dangerous," Guido said.

"He will offer you something to eat. Pizza, perhaps. Do not eat it. Don't eat or drink anything he might offer you. And, please don't kill him," Richard replied.

"I do not kill," Guido said. I'm a collector, not a murderer. I'll have the check signed tonight. It's made out to me. I'll go to the bank tomorrow as soon as it opens, and get three cashiers checks – one for me and one for the boss for two-hundred grand and one for you for six-hundred grand. I'll be back here tomorrow at ten, or a little after."

CHAPTER THIRTY-EIGHT

Moon Muenter had sent Doowite Jackson and Polly Kjelson out on three separate expeditions to try to find the escaped patient, Buford Parker. Each time they had returned without him and without having found any clue as to where he might be. They had located his ranch and house, they told Muenter, but it looked untended and there was no evidence that anyone was there. But they were not discouraged, they said, and thought that continuing the search was appropriate.

In truth, the two hospital employees had not been back to the ranch since Buford had slipped them each half a PCB. Instead they would either go to Polly's or Doowite's apartment and have sex. Polly, having lived in the south all her life harbored so many opinions about black people that she couldn't believe that she had become intimate with one and was slowly falling in love with him. All the time she and Doowite had worked at the hospital together, they had never even greeted each other, and to say that Polly was frightened of him understates the reality. She was terrified that if the opportunity ever arose, that he would rape her. Now she looked forward to their forays into bed where they made wild, very vocal love. Doowite had an enormous penis, and although Polly did not have much experience that would allow her to place him in a percentile group, she knew that it was probably eight inches longer than the little feller that Donny Ray possessed. Doowite was also tender. Although they made love in what she thought must be very primitive ways, he was always gentle with her.

On the return trip to the hospital, they would always stop at the soda fountain and get hot fudge sundaes.

They had gone out three consecutive days, and each time Muenter had told them to give it up – that they were wasting valuable time. All three times they had argued that they felt as if they were getting close. So Muenter would let them go again.

But today, their fourth, he told them no more. "I don't care if I ever see that son-of-a-bitch anyway. I didn't like him. That piece of shit thought that just because he was a Longhorns fan that I should be his buddy. Fuck that. Good riddance, I say."

So it looked like the beautiful affair between Polly and Doowite would have to end. As they left Muenter's office, Polly whispered to Doowite, "Come over after work tonight."

Doowite said nothing, but winked and smiled.

My, my, what teeth that man has, thought Polly.

After she left work, Polly stopped and bought what she thought was a nice bottle of wine. It wasn't, but they sipped it as though it was, as they sat anticipating another two-hour recreational romp. Half way through the bottle, Polly said, "You know, Doowite, I'm not quite as naive as you might think. For example, once in a while when me and my girlfriends get together, they will talk about good fucks and bad fucks, so I do know that there is some variation from fuck to fuck." Polly felt very sophisticated talking in this way. "I just wanted to tell you that you are probably the best fuck in the world. In the whole *world,* do you hear me? You know, I think that you and I should live together. If we combined our rent, we could get a real nice place – even buy a house. What do you think?"

"Yeah, we could do that."

"What fun that will be! How wonderful. We can look this weekend. Come on, Doowite. let's go into my bedroom and have one of those great fucks that is our specialty."

෨

Guido showed up at ten thirty the next morning with the three promised checks.

"Good work," Guido, Willy told him. Any glitches?"

"No… no, pretty routine."

Wilson then asked, "Anything? Anything at all? I mean he can't have just said, 'oh yes, fine, I should have paid Mr. Wilson a long time ago.'"

"No… no, it's never like that, but I have techniques, you know. Techniques. They always work. Almost always."

"Can you tell me what happened over there?"

"No… no, pretty routine. But yeah, when I got there he was sleeping. That *was* a little weird, because he was sleeping on the floor of the living room – butt naked. Yeah, that was weird. So I put my belt around his ankles. Not my belt, you know, but this ankle belt that I use. It's cool. Leather with Velcro. I could show it to you if you want." Guido looked at Rico, who showed no indication of wanting to see the cool belt. "So, anyway, that wakes him up. He's real nice. He says, 'I got something for ya.' Something like that, anyway. And so he goes into this pantry in his kitchen and he's there for, you know, less than a minute. And all of a sudden he goes bonkers. You know, berserk. I never seen anything like it. First he's angry. Then he comes out and he's crying, know what I mean? Crying. So I say 'the fuck's the matter?' and he says something about his balls. So yeah, that was weird. Very weird, know what I'm sayin'? Otherwise, pretty routine."

CHAPTER THIRTY-NINE

Betty Jane cooked some bacon and fixed an omelet for Michael. "Man, this is good stuff," Michael said.

"Thanks. Hey, do you ever go by Mike?"

"Yeah. A few people call me Mike. You like Mike better?"

"I do, actually. As long as you don't mind. What was the most dangerous thing you ever did?"

"I don't know. Let me think." After a few moments passed, Michael showed Betty Jane what appeared to be a burn on his hand.

"Is that a bullet hole?" she asked.

"No. I was flying a kite, and the kite got struck by lightening. Isn't that pretty much the way Benjamin Franklin did it? But he caught it in a jar, somehow."

"Yeah, a Leyden jar, whatever that is. I wonder how he knew what kind of jar to use. Anyway, getting back to you, so you're flying a kite and what, lightening strikes it and the electricity comes down the string and burns your hand?"

"Yep, that's pretty much it. I had just taken the kite from my son, who had been flying it. How lucky was that? I've always thought that it would have killed my son, who was four at the time."

"I thought the most dangerous thing you ever did would be something related to your job. I thought you might tell me the real story of the scar on your cheek."

"I did."

"I'm not sure I believe that."

"You don't need to. It doesn't matter."

"There's something else that comes to mind, Mike."

"What?"

"I didn't know you had a son."

"I don't."

"And the story about the lightning and taking the string from your son?"

"Well, I made up the part about my son."

"Did you make up the part about the kite, too?"

"Yes."

"How did you really get the scar?"

"I got it while boar hunting on Mount Parnassus."

"Mount Parnassus. Where is Mount Parnassus?"

"I believe it is in central Greece."

"What were you doing there?"

"As I said, I was boar hunting."

"Did you happen to run into Odysseus there?"

"No but I have heard that he met a similar fate."

Betty Jane looked at her new friend with a sense of affection that she had never in her life experienced. She smiled and he smiled back.

ॐ

Betty Jane passed the news to Tina and Paula that she was able to identify and separate the two batches of balls. There were four hundred seventy eight good ones and she didn't count the bad ones, but it looked like around five hundred. Betty Jane said that she was willing to divide them up three ways which would give them around a hundred fifty nine each. When she told Paula, Paula said, "I don't want that many, but I want some."

"How many do you want?"

After thinking for a brief moment, Paula said, "I want five."

"Five?"

"Yeah."

"I can bring them to your motel in a little jar. Will that work for you."

"Sure, that would be great. Thanks a lot, BJ."

"Are you sure that's all you want, Paula? You could probably sell them."

Paula thought again. "No. I'll take six. I'll give one to Karole. She's my good friend from the fishing trip in Argentina. You and Tina can have the rest. But hey, if any good stories come out of them, give me a call, okay?"

"I will."

"When can you bring me the specimens?"

"I can bring them to you this afternoon if you want."

"Perfect."

CHAPTER FORTY

A couple of hours later, Betty Jane knocked on Paula's motel room door and handed Paula the jar with the Pampas Cat balls in it.

"Want to come in for a glass of wine, BJ?"

"Why not. That sounds good."

Paula poured from a half full bottle of Argentine Malbec, and offered Betty Jane the vinyl covered chair. Paula sat on the edge of the bed. "I have a hunch that Richard will be leaving soon," Paula said.

"What makes you think that?"

"I talked to him again on the phone."

"You did?"

"Yeah, he had talked to Karole, the gal who was with me when we whisked Richard away from his Coast Guard pursuers. She was there when we used your pheromone to invite the cats to investigate Parker."

"Is that what happened? We never knew. Tina tells me that they're still puzzling over it at the hospital. What exactly happened?"

"We took all his clothes off and tied him to a tree. Then we put the pheromone all over his body. Within minutes we started hearing cats howling. We didn't stay around to watch."

"Is Richard in Austin like the feds think he is?"

"He is, but I don't know where. All he told me is that he's laying low for a few days."

"What's he here for, do you know?"

"He told me that he had business with Parker. He didn't tell me what it was."

"Wow, so the feds are right. God, I hope they don't catch him."

"Me too. He seemed pretty sure of himself when I talked to him, but he didn't tell me much. I don't know what his business with Parker is, but dollars to donuts it has to do with money."

"I don't think Tina knows any of this. Is it okay to tell her?"

"Sure, it doesn't give any clues about where he is. All I know is that he's layin' low."

"Wow, this is all pretty intriguing stuff. Listen, it's none of my business, but why did you want exactly five of the PCBs."

Paula didn't answer for several seconds as she thought about what she might say. Finally, she flushed almost imperceptibly and said, "True, BJ. It's none of your business. Maybe we can talk about it later."

"Right. I shouldn't have asked. I gotta go anyway. Keep in touch."

&)

Moments after Tina left, Paula's phone rang and she saw that it was Richard. She answered with, "Hey, Richard."

"Paula, Tomorrow at ten AM?

"Where?"

"Where are you?"

"I'm at the Longhorn Motel."

Richard consulted for several minutes with Willy and then asked Paula if she could see a Boot Barn across the street.

"Yes, I see it."

"Two blocks north of you, there's a Burger King. My friend Willy owns it. We'll meet there at ten, inside. What are you driving?"

"I've got a rented beige Jetta. See you there."

CHAPTER FORTY-ONE

When Robyn's phone rang the next morning, she saw that it was Bart. *What could he want?* she thought. *Yesterday we had one of the most incredible sexual experiences of all time. Will that ever be mentioned or acknowledged in any way? Could I have possibly predicted that in the middle of a high priority government mission I'd wind up spending almost an entire day screwing a married man who assigned himself to the task because his understudy had failed to perform up to FBI standards? Could I ever have predicted that I feel no remorse that I did? I still don't know what came over me, but I hope above hope that it does again sometime.*

All those thoughts having passed in a second or two, Robyn said, "Good morning, Bart."

"Good morning."

"Shall we meet for breakfast and discuss our strategy?"

"By all means, Admiral. How about Burger King?"

"Nine o'clock?"

"I'll meet you in the lobby at 8:30. We can walk," Bart said.

೮ಾ

"Tomorrow I leave, *Cuate.*"

"Hey, *amigo,* I was hoping you would stay."

"You know I can't. I'm *persona non grata* here in my own country."

"No shit, *Cuate.* How are you getting out?"

"That's arranged. Tomorrow I'm getting a ride to Galveston. From there I fly down to Monterrey with another friend, Anatolio Hernandez."

"I know Anatolio. You're in good hands, *mi amigo*. God, it's so great to see you. I'm glad you came by. Glad I could help you out, too."

Richard wondered how Willy knew Anatolio, but knew that it was a good time to be discrete."Me, too. I owe you one," he said.

"You owe me none, *cabron*. You already paid me. Listen, you need to make a couple changes in how you look. They're looking for you. For all you know they'll be having breakfast at my Burger King when you leave. Anyway, it's more than two hundred miles to Galveston. We'll just do a couple things. Once you're down to Monterrey you'll be okay."

&

The next morning, with black hair and a mustache, Richard made his way along the subterranean corridor to the stairway that ascended to the kitchen of the Burger King above. He got a cup of coffee and slid into a booth with a full view of the parking lot. In the booth adjacent to his, a couple was eating a BK croissan'wich. As he watched out the window for the beige Jetta, he heard the woman in the adjoining booth say *Parker.*

Just a coincidence, Ricardo thought, but shifted in his seat nervously. Now he kept his ears alert as he watched the window, hoping the Jetta would appear shortly. As he tried to listen, the voices dropped so that they were no longer audible.

&

"Whatever you do, don't look, Robyn. Keep looking at me. Keep your voice low."

"What's up?" Robyn said softly.

173

"I'm pretty sure the guy in the booth next to us is Wilson. I can't be positive because if it is, he's wearing a disguise."

"Have you got cuffs?"

"Yes," Bart said softly.

"Well, shouldn't you go over there and nail him?"

"Not now. One, I'm not sure it is Wilson, and two, I don't want to make a stir in here."

"I think you're making a mistake."

"You could be right, but we can see what happens. If he gets up to leave we can get him as soon as he's outside. One thing is that when he stands up we'll be able to tell if he's tall. Wilson is six-four."

"I'd get him now, Bart. He's right there."

"The guy has black hair and a mustache. Richard is blond, or at least, sandy blond."

"Can you see what he's doing?

"It looks as if he's maybe looking for something. He's got his eyes on the window."

"Someone is going to pick him up. This is our chance, Bart. I don't know why you don't go over there and cuff him. Ask the questions later."

"I'm just not sure. Imagine the scene if he's the wrong guy."

"Okay, your call. But put me on record as thinking you're making a big one here, Bart."

"It looks to me like the guy is trying to listen to what we're talking about. Let's cool it. I'll keep my eye on him. Be ready. If he leaves, we'll snag him outside the door."

"Okay, chief," Robyn said skeptically.

ഗ

Paula was late. Richard was starting to get nervous. No. panicky. He heard the name *Parker* at the adjoining table, and now they were talking in hushed tones. Had they spotted him? He considered making a run for it, but realized that would be stupid. At least the disguise he was wearing would make them a little bit uncertain. If they really were after him and they weren't at least a little bit uncertain, they would have confronted him by now. He kept his eye on the parking lot. *I have to spot her in the lot. I can run out and jump in the car before they can get me. If those two are really cops, or Coast Guard or whatever, I've got to get into the car before they can stop me.*

At that moment he saw a beige Jetta pull slowly into the lot. It turned into a parking slot right in front of the entry. *Shit,* Richard thought. *We'll never get out now. Well, it is what it is. It's now or never. Do or die. All or nothing. Let's see, can I think up any more clichés that fit the moment? Nothing else comes to mind. Be cool.*

Richard stood and walked nonchalantly toward the exit. Paula had gotten out of the vehicle and was starting to come in.

"It's him," Bart said softly. "Let's go."

As Richard exited, Paula saw him and took a step or two towards him as if she was going to hug him. Richard was frantically signaling her to get back into the drivers seat, but she apparently did not understand.

"Get back in," he finally said with evident urgency.

"Wilson?" he heard from directly behind him. Richard tried to open the passenger door but couldn't. *Godammit. It's locked.*

As soon as Paula heard Bart call out Wilson's name, she turned around and saw him taking cuffs out from behind his back. *"Wilson?"* she heard again.

In a move so quick that even Richard did not see how it was accomplished, Paula spun around and planted a right cross squarely on the side of Knowland's jaw. A frozen Robyn looked on like a marble statue as Knowland crumpled to the ground. *Oh my god,* she thought. *Billy Joe Bunch did not faint.*

175

Paula was back in the car on the driver's side as Richard, still agape, looked on in awe. "Get the fuck into the car, Rich," she said. "Get in."

Richard finally came out of his stupor and jumped in as Paula peeled out in the Jetta.

"Now they're going to be after both of us," Paula said with a grin.

When she hit the freeway, she ran it up to eighty miles per hour and headed for Buford Parker's ranch.

CHAPTER FORTY-TWO

"**W**hoever that lady back there was, she sure liked my right cross. As you know, the bolo is my usual knockout punch, but it's not like it's the only arrow in my quiver," Paula said.

"Is there something I should know about you, Paula?"

"Nope. Just that I know how to take care of myself."

As they pulled into Parker's place, Paula told Richard to slump down so Parker would not see him. It was not an easy thing to do for the tall man in a small car, but he managed to put the seat back in full recline and slide down.

"Wait here until I signal for you to come in," Paula said.

Buford Parker, still groggy from his most recent ingestion of half of a Pampas Cat testicle, was still as vigilant as his condition would permit. Watching the front walkway he saw the tall stately Paula approaching. She wore a skirt and blouse with western styling, and her flowing gentle curls blew softly in the breeze. *What have we here?* Buford wondered. *If beauty can be classified as classic, here it comes. There is something vaguely familiar about the face. Could it be that we had a romantic interlude? Oh my, what ever happened to my supply of huevos. Now is when I could really use one. My my, wouldn't those long legs fit nicely around my round little body.* The thoughts were still alive as he answered the doorbell. Paula did look lovely, and Buford did, indeed, vaguely recall the face from somewhere.

"Buford Parker – at your service, my dear." They were the only words he spoke. Paula's bolo punch caught him under the chin and he was on the floor instantly. Paula inserted the index finger of each hand into the corners of her mouth and whistled. Richard emerged from the Jetta and walked toward her.

"The jar. Get the little jar," she called.

Wilson returned to the car and got the small jar of PCBs. When he rejoined Paula, she had dragged Parker into his house and was removing his clothing. Paula had put the Pampas Cat balls into an ounce or two of vodka. When they had removed every stitch of clothing from the soft, pinkish body of Buford Parker, Paula held his mouth open, tilted his head back and said, "Pour em right on in."

Richard uncapped the little jar and poured the contents – five testicles – down Parker's throat. He had to depress Parker's tongue slightly to get the last two to go down, but down they went.

"We probably don't have a lot of time," Paula said. About the only place they know to look for us is here. I would love to see him regain conciseness, he'll probably break everything in the house trying to screw it." Even as she was talking, an enormous erection formed on the body of the otherwise comatose fat man.

Paula punched in 9-1-1 on Richard's throwaway phone and waited until the operator said, "Name and location, please."

Paula gave the address of Parker's house and said, "There is a man down here. He appears to be alive, but in critical condition. Please send an ambulance."

"May I have your name please?" demanded the operator.

"This is an emergency," Paula yelled "Send an ambulance ASAP. Make sure there's an EMT aboard. Thank you operator."

"What next?" Richard asked.

"As much as I'd like to find out what is next in the life of Buford Parker, I think we'd better beat a hasty retreat. You told me that a friend was going to fly you out of Galveston, right?"

"Right. I forgot I told you that."

"Well, you did, so I arranged a flight for myself back to Omaha from there. We have to make tracks, because my flight leaves in five hours. You'd better let your friend know that you want to leave as soon as we get there. It should take four hours from here."

Paula had mapped out a non-freeway routing for their departure from the ranch, reasoning that they might be pursued during this segment of their adventure. She was right. Ten minutes after they turned out of Parker's driveway, Robyn and Bart, the latter still a little groggy, turned in.

Richard called Anatolio Hernandez and told him to have his twin engine Cessna prepped for departure in four hours. Anatolio assured him that he would be ready. Richard removed the sim card from his phone, opened the car window, and threw the phone into the sun-baked sand along the highway.

"Too bad we can't be around to see what happens out at the ranch," Paula said.

"For sure." Richard said. "It will be an interesting scene. No doubt about that."

CHAPTER FORTY THREE

When the ambulance arrived at Parker's ranch, Robyn and Bart were still puzzling over the naked, torpid, but sexually ready Buford Parker. "We're too late," Robyn said to Bart. They've been here and gone."

"What in the hell?" said the EMT. "What did you do to this guy. I've never seen anything like this in my life. I'm going to have to get your names and make a report. I also have to call the police. There is some kind a crime here, although it defies any normal definition of a crime. What in the hell is going on. Did you two make the 9-1-1 call?

Robin showed her Coast Guard ID, and urged Bart to show his.

"Admiral? You're an admiral?" said the EMT.

"Yes. And this is Agent Knowland of the FBI. It is a crime scene and we're investigating. No need to call the police. We *are* the police."

"What kind of a crime would you say this is, if you don't mind my asking, the EMT asked.

"A weird one," Robyn said.

"It sure as hell is, Admiral. I've never seen anything like it. That little fat man has the biggest boner I've ever seen, and he isn't even awake to know it. You know there's a joke about a guy who never did see how big of a boner he got because when he started to get stiff, all the blood would run down there and he would pass out. I don't tell it very well. The guy I heard it from really knew how to tell that joke. There's another one about this Scottish guy on the eve of his wedding. He's wearing a kilt, you know?.."

"Hadn't you better get this guy to the hospital?" Robyn said.

"Oh yeah, what should I tell them?"

"Tell them that you responded to a 9-1-1 call and this is what you found."

"If that boner goes down I'll just have to tell them about it. Who knows? Maybe it won't."

"We will follow you in. We might be ten, fifteen minutes after you. We're going to poke around here for a little while – see if we turn up anything."

The EMT wrapped Parker in a blanket and with the help of his assistant placed him on a stretcher and carried him to the truck.

℥

Paula and Richard arrived at the Galveston airport in a little under four hours. As they approached the terminal, Richard spotted a twin engine Cessna warming up and guessed it was Anatolio Hernandez. It was in a secure area and it suddenly dawned on Richard that he was going to have to pass through the TSA inspection line.

"You must be returning the car here, right Paula?"

"Right."

"Listen, Paula. I don't know how I can ever repay you for all your help and clever ideas. You're a real peach. But I think my best bet is to get out here."

"I would never help a guy I didn't love and respect, Rich. Take care. If you need me, you can count on me. And one other thing. If you ever go back to the Riachuelo Gato, let me know. Those were the finest days of my life – maybe not counting today."

Richard kissed her on the cheek and waved as he jogged over to the fence where Anatolio would be able to see him.

181

Anatolio was doing a visual on the gasoline in the tanks when he looked up and saw Richard at the fence. He strolled over and tossed a picture tag over the fence to Richard, who had peeled off the mustache, but still had black hair. Richard looked at it. It looked very authentic, not unlike a tag he wore when he was flying. Anatolio took him to a gate with a single guard and said something that Richard could not hear. "Card please," the guard demanded.

Richard showed the document and the guard looked back and forth from the picture to Richard's face. Finally, he said, "Nice dye job," and opened the gate.

Ten minutes later they were poised at the end of the runway. The radio squawked, "Cessna four-one-eight-four-echo clear for takeoff." Anatolio extended and lowered the flaps, opened both throttles and was airborne within a minute.

"Monterrey bound," he said to Richard. "Start talking, my friend. I have to turn around as soon as we land, so we've got two and a half hours to hear about two and a half years. You better talk fast."

&

Paula's flight took off on schedule. Her one remaining PCB, destined to be a gift to Karole, did not trigger any surveillance machine and was safely tucked into her carry-on bag.

CHAPTER FORTY-FOUR

Tina Chevaria was on the emergency ward shift when the ambulance carrying Buford Parker pulled up to the unloading dock. The stretcher unfolded into a gurney which was wheeled to the emergency room. Tina and the duty intern pulled the gray wool blanket off from around Buford Parker's body.

"*What?*" Tina cried out.

"What?" said the intern.

"Uh, what do you make of this guy?" Tina said.

"He was this way when we found him," the EMT said. "Quit a boner, eh?"

Tina smiled. She discretely looked at Buford's jaw. Sure enough, there was a bruise developing and a slight dislocation in the TMJ. Tina believed she knew just what had happened, and she was right. Would she let on that she knew? Never in a million years. *This will stump the staff just like last time,* she thought. *I wonder how long he'll be in a coma. What will happen first, will he regain consciousness, or will that erection disappear? If he comes to and still has the erection, every woman nurse, every female patient, and every female staff member will be at risk. Shall I warn them? Nah. This will be fun. I have only known Paula for a week, but this definitely has her signature. What a genius. Wait til Betty Jane hears about this. I gotta call her on my break. It's the Hookem House tonight, for sure.*

AFTERWORD

Following is the final chapter of *Pampas Cat*

CHAPTER TWENTY-THREE

Nurse Practitioner Tina Chevaria had the 7:00 AM to 3:00 PM shift at Brackenridge Hospital in Austin. Her advanced training in trauma care did not prepare her for the unresponsiveness of Buford Parker. In consultation with Dr. Joseph Tranchini, she ran every diagnostic procedure they could think of as well as those suggested in the Merck and other manuals. Parker's eyes seemed locked in place.

At the end of her shift on the second day after Parker had been dropped at the hospital by Billups, Tina went to the Hook 'em House to meet her old college friend, Betty Jane Griffin. They ordered Margaritas and after a half-hour or so of bouncing around different subjects, Tina mentioned the patient she was caring for. Without pointing out his trance-like condition, Tina described the scratches that covered his body. Betty Jane asked what his name was. Whether it was ESP, female insight, or her memory of Buford's fear of Frenzy, she somehow had a sense that it was Parker Tina was talking about.

"His name is Parker," Tina said. "Buford Parker." "Oh my God... unbelievable! I can't even begin to believe it. I know that man. Pink-skinned roly-poly guy, right?"

"That's him. How in the world do you know Parker, for goodness sakes?"

"It's a long story, Tina. The short version is that I did some research for him." Betty Jane sipped her margarita and considered how much she should reveal to Tina. She and Tina had been room-mates at Texas Tech and had enjoyed some magnificent frolics together, but they had let the friendship drift, and now Betty Jane didn't think the whole truth was appropriate. Besides, she still didn't know the whole truth herself. Her last experience with the so-called aphrodisiac was by far the worst night of her life.

"What kind of research?"

"It had to do with pheromones. That's all I really know. He was attempting to reproduce a pheromone. I think it might have had something to do with pesticide development. Something like that anyway. He's a strange bird, that's all I know."

"I wouldn't know. He's in a trance."

"A trance? What do you mean by a trance?"

Tina told Betty Jane about Parker's admission to the trauma clinic and described his state of suspension.

Betty Jane found the discussion puzzling, but in spite of her aroused curiosity she didn't want Tina to know anything about Pampas cat testicles or the strange relationship that she had had with Parker. Recalling the near-death experience the evening of their anticipated romp made her feel nauseous right then. She licked an inch of salt off the rim of her glass.

"Tina, I gotta get out of here. God, let's not wait a year until we get together again. This has been great, but I'm not feeling so good."

ॐ

On the fourth day after his arrival, Tina decided to look in on Parker before she left the hospital. When she peeked in the door she saw Buford sitting on the edge of his bed. "Where in the hell am I?" he asked her, almost shouting. Then his head flooded with the image of the several hours before he lost consciousness. Tears formed in his eyes and he began to sob.

"Mr. Parker, you need to get back in bed. I'll call Dr. Tranchini."

"Who the fuck is that?" Buford sobbed. "Oh God," the image returned. There were fourteen or fifteen cats all screaming and fucking his body at once. Two were on his face, one with its claws dug into his eyes. Buford convulsed and felt hot, acrid fluid from his stomach fill the back of his throat. He swallowed painfully. "Where am I?" he said again. "Am I still in Argentina? Thank the Lord I'm not outside. Oh, you would not believe what I've been through." It occurred to Buford that it might be advisable for him to be scarce with the realities of his experience. Nobody would believe it anyway.

"You're in Austin, Mr. Parker. You were brought in by a man from the Coast Guard station in Galveston. He said that you had an accident in Argentina, but he wasn't able to tell us any more than that. We asked him a lot of questions but he had no answers. Apparently he was ordered to bring you here, but wasn't told how you got injured. You must tell us whatever you can remember so we'll know how to proceed."

"I do remember I was going down to Argentina with the Coast Guard. They didn't know it, but I was going to kill a guy down there. Now that's something I shouldn't be talking to you about, so forget I ever said it. Beyond that I can't remember a thing."

Frightened, Tina said, "You'll have to excuse me, Mr. Parker, while I go and get Dr. Tranchini."

When she returned with the doctor, Buford was gone. "I swear, Doctor, he was sitting in extreme discomfort on the edge of the bed. He was disoriented, but conversant. He might have been hallucinating."

At that moment, the bathroom door opened, and Buford emerged without his hospital gown. His pink, moist skin was oozing blood and other exudates in spite of partial healing. His pubic area was heavily scratched and his penis barely visible. "Where the hell are my clothes? I want to get out of this God forsaken place. I've got business to take care of."

"Hold your horses, Mr. Parker," said Tranchini. "You're going nowhere at least until tomorrow. You were in serious trauma. You were in a state of suspended animation. Your symptoms were not interpretable. They were coma-like in some ways, but more akin to shock. And look at your body. It's a little surprising that you can even move. We will need to conduct some tests before we release you. Heretofore, we've had our hands tied because you were in a coma. About all we could do was cleanse and disinfect your wounds. We have sutured your nasal septum and done reconstructive work on your ear. One eardrum is perforated. Mr. Parker, I have never seen anything like this before. Your lacerations and puncture wounds are not healing as they should, and we need to know how you got them in order to guide us through the treatment process. Your wounds are consistent with what I've seen in gang-rape cases, but you must give us the details of how this happened."

"What the hell did you say your name was? Get me my clothes, damn it! Do you even know who you're dealing with?" Parker grabbed the bed spread and threw it around his shoulders. *These idiots wouldn't help me if I was a nun. I've got to change hosses here.* "Listen, this is your lucky day. Do you play the lottery? Well, you just won it without even buying a ticket. I've got a little gift for each of you that will make you beholden to me for the rest of your natural lives. You just need to get me out to my ranch."

"Mr. Parker, I'm going to call security if you don't cooperate. Now, please calm down."

"I'm the calmest one here. Now, get me my clothes and my personal effects so we can get the hell out of here and get out to my ranch. Keep in mind that I am Buford Parker. Parker extended his index and little fingers downward. "Hook 'em baby. It don't make a shit if Hicks *does* bail out on us. We're going to win the conference." He turned to Tina. "Miss, you are about to have an afternoon that you will never forget. Tell 'em at the desk out there that you're taking a sick day, or whatever." And to Tranchini, "Doctor, you can fuck your tests. You send somebody after my personal shit, and get ready to enjoy one of the most remarkable treats available to man."

"I'll get your stuff," Tranchini said to Parker, at the same time shooting a glance at Tina.

"Now, that's better," Parker said. "You're not as dumb as I thought." After Tranchini left the room Parker said to Tina, "You are about to experience the most unforgettable evening of your life. I hope you like our friendly doctor because by the end of the evening you are going to know him in ways that you haven't ever in your life even dreamed of as a possibility. And, believe it or not, it's all going to be enabled by cat balls. Cat balls. You probably think you didn't hear me right, but that's what I said. Cat balls. More specifically Pampas cat balls.

When Dr. Tranchini returned, he was accompanied by two orderlies in white. They had Parker buckled into the straight jacket in seconds. He struggled against them, but it caused him so much pain that he succumbed. As they escorted the squealing, kicking fat man from the room Tina stood shaking her head. *A party enabled by cat balls? The most unforgettable evening of my life? Wait until Betty Jane hears this one!*

Made in the
USA
Lexington, KY